D0934659

Being Here

Being Here

Stories

Manini Nayar

UNIVERSITY PRESS OF KENTUCKY

Editorial and Sales Offices: The University Press of Kentucky
663 South Limestone Street, Lexington, Kentucky 40508-4008
www.kentuckypress.com

Cataloging-in-Publication data available from the Library of Congress

ISBN 978-0-8131-8252-0 (hardcover : alk. paper)
ISBN 978-0-8131-8253-7 (pdf)
ISBN 978-0-8131-8254-4 (epub)

This book is printed on acid-free paper meeting
the requirements of the American National Standard
for Permanence in Paper for Printed Library Materials.

Manufactured in the United States of America.

Member of the Association
of University Presses

To Nitin, Avi, Ro, and Taran,
&
in memory of my parents,
A. P. Balakrishnan Nayar and Sarada Nayar,
with love

Contents

Home Fires

I

When Timothy McVeigh was sentenced to death for the bombing of the Murrah Building in Oklahoma City, Krishnakant Sharma was trying to lace up his boots. Good boots they were, too, from the Walmart in the plaza a few blocks away: brown, strong, and stiff with a polyurethane finish that suggested these weren't boots at all, but luggage in disguise. Sharma didn't like his boots. He felt a stranger in them, an inhabiter of space designed for more purposeful insteps, those that trod the streets of Manhattan as if to say "Outta my way" or "Giddadahere" or other confident assertions that remained the prerogative of real Americans. All Sharma could muster was a squeaky "Excuse me" when women of formidable posteriors rested shopping bags against his ankles in the rush-hour subway, at which remonstrance they glared at him pitilessly.

Sharma did not think much about these things. He was a man given to simple attentions, immediate and in need of correction—a lock of hair against his brow, a slipcover on the sofa slightly askew, a toothpaste tube bereft of toothpaste top, a pair of uncooperative boots.

On the television screen, images came and went. People sobbed. A lawyer in a wheelchair beamed, radiating success. Reporters spoke intensely, their hair at coiffed attention. Then came an advertisement for Pepsi crowded with cavorting children. Sharma's eyes misted, thinking how much he loved America. God Save the Queen, thought Sharma, substituting in his mind's eye the Statue of Liberty for any contending monarch. More queenly she, and silent, too. Much like Mataji, his mother, the matriarch back home in India, wielding her rolling pin over chapati dough, the fairy godmother of his gastronomic pleasures. Give her an eggplant and she could transform it into spicy bhurtha, pumpkin could metamorphose into sabzi, all with a wave, a stir of her magical kitchen ladle. An image of Disney World rolled into view, knocking aside the Statue of Liberty. Sharma shook himself gently. He was inhabiting too many realities, as usual.

"Excuse me!" said a voice, not like Sharma's "Excuse me" at all, but a subway woman's "Excuse me." The voice ran like rolling trash cans across his vision of Disney World.

"Yes?" said Sharma doubtfully. He distrusted voices, especially if they were disembodied. Sometimes they spoke to him in his sleep at night, and he would surface clutching a pillow as if it were a raft, riding the seas of his terror. Those voices were deeper, though, calling the name of his dead wife, deep voices thinning as he came to consciousness, heavy ropes of sound shrinking to mice tails, to shoelaces, to slivers of sound. And then Sharma was alone in the silent apartment, the air still and clear as standing water, a comforting thought if he could swim. But he could not, and, helplessly sinking, he felt the waters close over his head until he flung himself from bed to table lamp to open window to gulp down the indifferent air.

"I'm lacing up my boots," called Sharma defensively. He recognized the voice, having met it a day earlier rising up the stairs to him without remorse, the voice of Ms. Kaminsky ("Call me Ann") on the second floor, all the way from Nantucket to a tiny office on 43rd Street, where it existed with equally unapologetic voices in freeform cacophony. The voice of "You're so quiet" Ann, Ann of the thousand jeers, who had scoffed him into a dinner invitation tonight. "Not a date," she had warned him, "just a food-thing. I like looking at a face while I'm eating—helps my digestion."

Sharma did not want to meet Ann.

He opened the door, his laces still at odds. His feet were splayed, set apart from each other in disgrace, his work unfinished.

"Lacing up your boots?" inquired the rest of Ann as she entered the room.

Sharma searched for an airy riposte but found none.

He bent guiltily and began retying his boots, a hurricane of fingers at work. The hurricane intensified. It sped all the way up to Sharma's head and whirled his thoughts around. Statue of Liberty. Mataji. Disney World. *Is she laughing at me?*

"Funny little guy," volunteered Ann, contemplating the geometric angles made by Sharma's skinny frame as it stooped and tugged. She watched his feet pull and protest. "You could tie those laces any which way. Do they have to be exactly the same length on each foot?"

Toothpaste tube bereft of toothpaste top. Slipcover askew.

"I'm a perfectionist," admitted Sharma. He said this in the bright-happy way he had heard television anchors address one another. He hoped he had made a little joke. Ann did not laugh. She was watching TV.

"How depressing," said Ann. "You know what the verdict is—he's guilty. Now switch it off already. Don't wallow."

McVeigh's sister sobbed in an unrestrained way. A lawyer raised an eyebrow, mentioned conspiracy. Words flew from his mouth like bats, dark, winged, secret.

Sharma found his voice. It had been lurking somewhere in his chest, slipping down into his feet, scurrying out onto the carpet. It came back squeaking but still there.

"No, no," he protested, "I just turned on the television to check on tomorrow's weather. It seemed like rain."

"Oh yeah?" said Ann. Not a question but a jeer.

Sharma and Ann walked down the winding staircase until they hit hard gravel. The earth beneath their feet was full of little stones, sharp and mean. *Like your eyes,* thought Sharma, smiling nervously at Ann.

"Wrong shoes," said Ann, grimacing. She wobbled slightly in her blue pumps with round vents at the sides. Portholes. Then she righted herself. "Where to? Indian?"

"Why not?" said Sharma, feeling gallant for no reason. He was hungry. For breakfast he'd had a dispirited banana. No lunch. Sharma missed the smell of puris cooking in hot oil, of cauliflower and eggplants sizzling in masala. Here the smell of food was sanitized, banished into the recesses of microwave platters, arising, if at all, like old sponges filled with vegetable rot. He usually held his nose when he ate, a sign of surrendered respect for the rubbery thing on his plate and a tribute to the memory of evenings in Dehradun under the jacaranda tree, its flowers casting a fragrance over the richness of the meal, in benediction.

"To eat well is to sense divinity," offered Sharma, hoping that his aphorism might suggest to Ann his hidden troves of wisdom.

Ann laughed, though it was no joke.

"Funny man," she said. "Though I guess a lot of you guys back in India are starving. So it makes sense—sort of."

"No, no," said Sharma, "not what I meant at all. Besides, India now has a surplus grain production. We just don't distribute it evenly."

"What are you talking about?" demanded Ann. And Sharma wondered, too.

II

When Sharma killed his wife, he did it the same way he might brush his teeth, with familiarity and a sense of routine. He did it slowly, day by day, releasing from under her floating life the certainties of her existence, until she sank, imperceptibly, without struggle, into a stagnation without undertow, a complete stillness of the spirit. She had come to him, after all, an unfinished thing, a child bride, almost colorless except for her red bindi and her hennaed hands. He had accepted her into his life the way a dog might walk into his yard, a loping interruption to be chased away or fed, whatever his mood demanded. Marriage wasn't so much an intrusion as a letting out of his life, like the hem of old trousers, or a sneeze.

And when the smoke was thick and the air so hot she couldn't breathe, that kind of ending was only the coda to a life already lost. Sharma was not responsible for the theater of her departure—of that he was sure—but only for the acts, the moments, that ascended like stairs toward the climax. The burning ghats. The funeral pyre. The kerosene stove. Variations on an old and sacred myth, mutable and appropriate for the times. Sharma despised melodrama. But he understood the scaffolding beneath it. All it took was his silence and contempt, and from Mataji the stray beating, outpourings of resentment, tirades on dowryless women. Still. You did not die for words. And if you did, the fire was in your hands, the match self-struck. Mataji and he were bystanders, fanners of flames perhaps, but empty-handed, palms held upward for inspection. "No, Inspector Banerjee, I was out of the house at the time. My mother was rolling chapatis on the verandah. The servants were asleep. . . ."

III

The one time Sharma felt a need for love in his marriage was on the day after the wedding when it was apparent that this union was a mistake. Here he was, so mild-mannered a man that he was used to being often pushed around and even bullied, so immersed in his work, so tended by a hovering mother, that nothing seemed lacking. The well-meaning aunts, the nosy neighbors, whispering, rustling, "A good education, a good job, and not yet married? No son to carry the family name?" Then Mataji's eyes red with sudden longing. "A grandson—my only wish, my desire for you, all I have ever asked." So before long Aradhana, fatherless, stepmothered, the sort whose hair he might have tousled, whose cheek patted, so young was she. Now she was thrust upon him, and he recoiled, not so much from her as from the demands of his existence. Husband. Father. Breadwinner. For a woman he had not chosen. He looked for a partner, an equal. Not a child seeking shelter. Yet he could not deny his mother her heart's desire, deny his own son a birth.

But one day, a year after his wedding, while lounging in a deck chair shelling peanuts on an October afternoon, Sharma was startled by a premonition. He felt a need larger than his entire being loom before him. He couldn't tell what it was or where it had come from. He could not swat it away. It had no shape or form but simply loomed. One step forward and there it was, blocking his way. Two steps back and it followed him so that he could have tipped into the rose bushes (had he any) in the garden. The importance of putting the nebulous into words, Sharma knew, was to give it expression and therefore to reshape it, destroy the original, make it subject to his control. The use of language could make the djinns disappear.

He attempted to phrase his fears to Mataji.

"There is something that bothers me," said Sharma to his mother.

Mataji's eyebrows rose and fell, twin arcs of alarm.

"Is it Aradhana?" Surely it was Aradhana. Dowryless daughter-in-law. Eater of our foods. Partaker of our lives. Wombless parasite. Mataji's sari—always white in deference to Ranmol, dear departed husband and father—was as crisply starched as her voice.

"It is not Aradhana," Sharma said carefully, "it is because of Aradhana."

Mataji pondered the distinction.

"Whore," she offered.

Sharma shifted with irritation. He could see the looming in front of him and realized with some fear that he had erred. The named thing can become the name. The word draws the image and the image threatens you, becomes the master. What should he do? The looming was gray, thick, and advancing.

"I do not care for Aradhana," said Sharma, embarrassed to use a stronger word. "Marriage to her has shown me what my future lacks." Aradhana of the light complexion and brown eyes, button nose and long straight hair. The singer of classical songs and baker of English pound cakes. The thumper of Kuchipudi feet. Slim-hipped and child-less Aradhana, her womb empty with the secret invasions of growths and tissues. Dowryless but beautiful. And not loved. Not by Sharma. Not by Mataji. The dog yelping at the gate.

Mataji's eyes grew fond. Wives were not to be loved but endured like a menstrual headache. Her own husband had not loved her, nor she him. But the Dear Departed had given her a son who was hers and hers only.

Sharma gazed at his mother, at her angularity in heart and bone, and understood that he was captive. He began to see that the gray mass was of his own making, the part of him that had struggled to leave years ago when he was a child, to shape a life of immense possibilities. And now it was back, looming, threatening, the epitaph of his desires. It moved toward him as Mataji smiled and smiled, eyebrows arched like the lifted folds of a vampire's cape.

IV

"The trouble with you Indians," said Ann, poking a piece of chicken around her plate, "is that you don't know when to stop."

She meant the spices in her food, robust and dangerous, too consuming for a palate raised on meatloaf and boiled peas. Salt might be added, a flick of pepper. Not an avalanche of powders.

Sharma stared at her guiltily. *What do you mean? We never touched her. Not a bit. Notatall.*

"What are you jumping at?" demanded Ann. "Are you paying attention? Don't be a bore—I can't sit here with someone who has nothing to say."

Her voice seemed serrated, as if she had done him a favor by inviting him to a corner restaurant, this little fellow with a hairline far from shore and outsized ugly boots. If Kevin had still loved her, hadn't written "It's over" on the back of a grocery bill and slipped it under her door, if he hadn't answered her telephone calls with "Sorry, this is the laundromat" and slammed the receiver down as she (in various tones and verbal arrangements) pleaded for him to talk to her. If she hadn't realized that Kevin Jamison had four women, each in a different borough of New York City, two others called Ann and one, mysteriously, Pompanola—*then*. *Then* she wouldn't be here with this idiot gnawing on chicken bones.

"I was merely allowing you to enjoy your dinner," said Sharma, looking into her pebble-sharp eyes. "I thought conversation might distract you from savoring the subtleties of the spices."

Who talks like that? thought Ann. *Savoring the subtleties of the spices. Talk English.*

"What's in the spinach?" said Ann. "It's too stringy."

"Coriander," he said untruthfully.

"Well, it's just weird." said Ann. She seemed close to tears. Sharma roused himself in some surprise at this unexpected character reversal. He offered her the dal and roti. He spoke at length about the wonders of New York City. The Met. The Brooklyn Bridge. The Statue of Liberty. A true monarch, who could never peddle helicopter books.

Ann allowed herself a twitch of the jaw, suggesting amusement. A joke! A joke! exulted Sharma, as if sighting an elephant on a bus. He leaned a little closer.

"All is good?" asked the waiter, hovering asplike. He moved in coils, a sudden spin and he was gone, another and there he was.

"Verygood, verygood," said Sharma. "Check please."

When the check arrived, Sharma waved away Ann's contribution. "No, no. Allow me. My pleasure."

"But I invited you," said Ann.

"Mypleasure, mypleasure," said Sharma, fumbling for his limp black money pouch, the weight and color of his fortunes.

"Better be getting back," remarked Ann. "My boyfriend Kevin might be waiting. He's kind of weird that way." Just in case Sharma had any ideas.

Sharma felt an immense relief: he was not to be appropriated. A cannonball hurtling toward him had turned to cotton wool and could be blown away. Ann noticed his lack of disappointment. Kevin. Of the spiked blond hair. Versed in Keats and Kant. An architect with all the savvy of the professional class. She saw the holiday flat in Cape Cod slip away. The nights at Carnegie Hall. Pompanola—what kind of name was that? It brought to mind the bulls running in Spain. And this dried stalk of a man. No, he couldn't possibly not be disappointed.

"Your boots are hideous," she said furiously, fighting the bile that arose in her after the pinch of after-dinner somf stuck in her gullet like sand. Bitter that he relished his thumb-and-index-finger portion. Always the one left out. "I'm saying this as a friend. Don't go to job interviews in those boots. Nobody buys this stuff except you immigrants." Who can't tell the good from the bad. In shoes. In food. In women. "I might still have an old pair you could use—one of Kevin's. He has more than he knows what to do with."

Sharma thought how easy it would be to squeeze her throat. It would feel like a sack with the rice running out. The thought struck him effortlessly as a siren wailed down the sun-blushed night.

V

When Aradhana was eight years old, her mother gave her an oblong box with chocolates of varying sizes and middles. The gift was a stretch, because Mami was a health fanatic who read health food journals with the kind of reverential humility reserved for audiences with the Pope and, without exception, considered chemical additives in food an act of Satan. Being used to an improving diet of cabbage and dal with rice, Aradhana was naturally suspicious. On the box were the words "Black Magic" printed in a script that Aradhana mistook for a code. "Read between the ridges of the alphabet," whispered Aradhana's secret friend, Neema, who lived partly in her head and partly in the branches of the peepul tree outside Aradhana's bedroom window. The tree was Satan's hand rising out of the earth in a clutch of gnarled fingers ringed with leaves.

"Get there," Aradhana would say sternly to Neema, "and don't come back until you can behave!" And out crept Neema and shivered among the satanic leaves until Aradhana took pity and let her back in. Neema stole sugar from the pantry. She lied about brushing her teeth in the morning. She was the one who painted Meena Auntie's chair with chalk. *Target practice,* whispered Neema to Aradhana, who couldn't go that far. Not when Mami's eyebrows rushed together into a black arrow, thick and unforgiving. "Get there!" Mami would shout, pointing to Aradhana's bedroom, "and don't come out until you can behave!"

Aradhana feared the power of mothers, especially if, like hers, they were of the ersatz variety, her own having died of cancer seven years ago. A steppie. A fairy badmother. Eyebrowed and pointy-fingered. A fountain of black hair steepled on her head for a hat. When Aradhana married, it would be to a man who chased the witch away, banished her forever into the Tree of Satan where she could eat Black Magic chocolates until her eyes went bad and her teeth dropped out. Then the chastened leaves would fall from the tree like stars, cascades of triumphant light.

Aradhana scoured the surface of the chocolate box, and the longer she looked, the clearer it became to her. From between the spaces of the alphabets on the box arose another text: "Kill the Girl." ("That's what it says," agreed Neema. "She wants you dead.")

"Hates me, hates me, hates me," whispered Aradhana to Neema on nights when the wind barely turned and the moon's crescent swung insouciantly like banter. "But I'm going to marry a prince and change her into horse dung." Overhead, the sky spun on spiderwebs of light.

Neema nodded sagely inside Aradhana's head. Up and down, up and down went her head, and Aradhana counted the nods instead of sheep until she fell asleep, one hand outstretched, palm upward, to trap the falling stars and leaves.

But in the morning, when she awoke, Aradhana was alone, because Mami smacked her ears if she caught the girl speaking aloud to herself. "Only low-class people do such stupid things," warned Mami. "Remember you are a Cariappa." Being a Cariappa also meant that you ate with a fork and knife, not your fingers. Even a chapati had to be sliced into neat rectangles before being lifted mouthward. Being a Cariappa meant that you smiled at Mami's friends (including

Meena Auntie, now impervious to smiles) and recited Wordsworth with Mami's distant notion of a British accent ("Ai wonded leunli ezzei klawd"), after which performance the Aunties clapped without enthusiasm. Aradhana had to practice her diphthongs. Poorly enunciated diphthongs proved that you were only pretending to be upper class and that all the fork-and-knife chapati eating was a sham. So Aradhana practiced daily in front of her mirror. "Deah me! Doo ai see ei baicycle in the bau-gen-villa bush?" and other such diphthong-rich phrases Mami had jotted down on scraps of paper as self-improving exercises.

Daddy, mustachioed and portly, wasn't there to monitor Aradhana's improvements. Mostly he was in Darjeeling on tea business. He was the best tea taster in the world, thought Aradhana, and when she married her prince, Daddy would be Chief Horseman of the Stables and sweep away the night's refuse. Then he would burn the dung into ash which Aradhana would apply to her cheeks with fork and knife. ("Animal manure, well incinerated, is effective in closing open pores," Aradhana had read in Mami's health journals.) After which she and Daddy and the prince would drink tea, Mami now pressed into cosmetic service.

But Daddy had other ideas, and when Aradhana was sixteen, he ran away with the music teacher in the elementary school, leaving Mami and Aradhana staring at each other across the dinner table late one evening, wondering why they should live together anymore since their only known connection was on a boat to Hong Kong singing "Goodnight, Irene." Stay she did, with Neema-in-her-head for company; school until four in the evening, Kuchipudi class until six, after which it was dinner, homework, bed.

And at night when the moon's crescent lightened and swung, Aradhana would climb onto her windowsill and look through the peepul leaves into the black wash of sky to ponder the image of her life. The father who had left, serenading; the ear-smacking steppie now permanently shuttered behind a bedroom door; even the girl in her head who grew fainter with time. It struck Aradhana as she sat balanced on her windowsill between earth and sky that this moment of dormancy, the pause between things, the space between the Black Magic alphabets, was a good enough place. If this were a language, it was not of laughter or enlightenment, but a wordless language of absence, of silence and endurance. A language like no other, of her own encoding. If she held her breath, she would become that pause, that space, when life seemed suspended in its own longing, nothing existing, everything possible, like an imminent birth. And, flexing like a wing lifting and falling, she felt her heart flow into the waiting darkness. Released, she was comforted.

That is, until she married Chotu Sharma ten months later, lit a kerosene stove, and burned.

VI

"Well, I guess we'll do this again," said Ann gaily, astonishing Sharma with yet another character cartwheel.

He looked at her, at her thin long face scarred with a patch of acne, her little eyes and absurdly genteel, slender neck. Her puffs of tobacco-brown hair billowing about her shoulders. All this time she had been the Voice, the Jeer. Now he saw legs, arms, an entire history waiting to well up and spill. In four short blocks he'd already been introduced to Ann's Aunt Marian with angina, Ann's bouts with asthma, her parents who summered in the Berkshires, and a dog called Fred who had, apparently, adopted the family during a camping trip to Yosemite when Ann was ten. Sharma had no wish to learn more, but he could sense the rumble beneath his feet, the earth trembling. His heart sank.

"Oh yes," said Sharma helplessly.

"Next time I'll treat," said Ann. "I only let guys I date pay for dinner." (Kevin. A grocery bill. He'd never paid. Lies. Lies.)

"A good strategy," agreed Sharma, wondering what that meant.

Sharma and Ann stared at each other for a moment before she said, "I know an Italian place. It's a bit of a walk but worth the effort."

Sharma saw stories rushing at him, street by street, tooting their horns.

"Maybe next week," Sharma began to say, but they had already arrived at the lobby of their apartment building, a small checkerboard room with a hatstand and a curved front desk behind which sat, without specific purpose, sad men of indeterminate origin. They seemed required to be there, on call, rather like Sharma now with Ann. At Sharma's approach, they disappeared, as if magically absorbed into the wainscoting. Sharma wished, briefly, for a similar fate.

He began his goodbyes by smiling uncertainly, extending a hand and clearing his throat.

"I can come up for a moment," said Ann quickly, ignoring Sharma, "in case you need to chat."

Sharma's room was the way he had left it except for a window that had mysteriously swung open. (Sharma checked for burglars. One can never be too careful.) He reached for his coffee pot, hoping Ann might be repelled by the stains necklaced around the bottom.

"My coffee pot's the same way," said Ann. "I don't always find the time to wash things up. Busy, busy, busy."

Ann and Sharma sat sipping coffee from mugs that said CALIFORNIA! SURF'S UP, DUDE!

For a moment, Sharma considered Ann with a completely detached tenderness. Her bony hands, refugee-thin shoulder blades. Now she was the one who was all angles. Sad, geometric Ann.

The television was still on, framing a network anchor talking so earnestly he might have been sincere. Still Oklahoma City. Interviews again. Friends. Coworkers. Lawyers.

"Switch that off," said Ann. "Let's talk."

Sharma felt a mass barreling toward him, a crush of words. He could sense it the way a dog anticipates an eclipse, how it runs from room to room looking for the source of its unease, how it cowers as the sky clenches and implodes and darkness fills the room. At this moment he wearied, wishing for nothing but a pause released from time in which he might lie low until the world was righted. He wanted no explanations or evasions or slanted light in which the truth moved sinuously, jumping from shade to shade.

So he said to Ann very simply, as if a perfectly logical connection extended between this evening and his past, this moment and all moments: "I was once married. My wife burned to death. She died from flames from a kerosene stove." Said that way, it sounded like a jingle ("And THAT'S the way to LAM-beth!").

At first it struck Sharma that Ann had nothing to say. Or that she hadn't heard. She seemed puzzled, then what may have been a confused recognition knitted her eyebrows. She began breathing harder, asthmatic in her fog.

After a minute, while knowledge and disbelief crossed and recrossed her face, her voice came out squeaky thin.

"A kerosene stove? Is this a joke?" she demanded, and when Sharma simply gazed at her, she said, "Omigod Omigod!"

Then she stood up the way women with large shopping bags in the subway stand up, purposeful but in disarray.

"I saw stuff like this on *60 Minutes*," she said. "You people don't really do this, do you? You couldn't have done it."

Ann sat down heavily, a sack with the rice running out.

"She died a year ago," said Sharma politely. "Burnt over most of her body." Wombless Aradhana.

Sharma looked at the clock. Later than he'd thought, 9:25. Turning around, he noticed that Ann was on her feet again.

"You make me sick," she said, and in fact she did look sick. Her face seemed green, or perhaps it was the streetlight through the slats that refocused the room, gave it depth and character, dramatized corners, mellowed furniture, allowed the room its theater of subtlety and intrigue.

Sharma could see that there wouldn't be an Italian dinner. Or any more of Aunt Marian's angina and Fred. He felt unexpectedly cheated, as if the weight of an anticipated burden had been stolen from him. He wanted it all back. Disdain. Kevin's boots. Coriander in the spinach. The Voice in cacophony.

But Ann had left, slamming the door, the coffee pot gurgling in glee.

Sharma sat on the bed and considered his next move.

"Joothe utharo," Mataji had always said when he entered the house. Remove your shoes. Show respect.

Sharma bent obediently and began the ritual wrestling with his boots.

When he was done, he noticed that the television program had cut to a commercial and a small white doughboy appeared, chortling when a huge finger pressed into his belly. Sharma smiled back, but the doughboy was gone, skipping, hopping over cinnamon rolls.

Having changed into his pajamas, Sharma wandered into the bathroom for a tube of toothpaste. He found it, top askew, and frowned.

As he brushed his teeth, it struck Sharma that the bathroom mirror was like a television set. He paused and postured in different network styles, then lifted up his toothbrush for a microphone. Behind him flames shot skyward as the Murrah Building crashed and fell. Sharma reported it all in a deep and somber voice, manly but sensitive. Heartened by his performance, he combed his hair, parting it neatly in the middle. But his hair stuck up like dry grass, scratching at the emptiness of air.

VII

A few years later, clear across the country when his immigrant vigor was chastened by a slowly balding pate and spongy waistline, Sharma drove a blue Mustang down another street in another city—this time in a black suit and leather pumps, briefcase by his side. Shoes that were shoes. Luggage, luggage. A salesman for computer software, Sharma now had a mortgage and a pension plan, two televisions and a fridge with an ice maker. A golden-haired (with some chemical help) wife and a stepson who tossed baseballs at him and called him Dad. Sharma had an American accent, except for vowels that hiccoughed awkwardly in sudden words, so that his wife's midwestern

parents sometimes gazed at him as if deciphering a conundrum—
What did he say? The calves are blue? The cars are blue?—their silver
heads bent in confusion, Sharma hot with shame.

As he steered the car through the dimming suburban lawns and
the hum of evening sprinklers, anticipating microwaved fish and
tater tots for dinner, his stomach a-growl, Sharma heard over the
radio a news flash that McVeigh had come to the end of his appeals.
There was talk of the Murrah Building, its rubble and horror. More
interviews. Tears. And the image of another burning came unbidden
to mind, rising like a fuming harpy. For a moment Sharma felt a kick
in his heart that was almost love, but he saw it just in time as a trick
in timing, a jolt so unseemly its rise and fall might someday be mistaken for grief.

The Secret Women of Vietnam

Somewhere out in the darkness sat a chubby man with a pug. Of this she had no doubt, no doubt whatsoever. A chubby man with a head as promising as a tree, bursting with new inventions like cherry blossoms in the spring. Of this she had no doubt. None at all. In the palm of her hand, her fate was written years ago at birth—before that even, somewhere in the womb. In the time before consciousness, her hands splayed out, revealing the lines that her life was to trace into being.

You will meet a man with two children and a temperament weak for sweetmeats and classical music.

The palmist had not mentioned the pug.

The pug would come after, a footnote with a tail.

But you had to believe the story as it was told, as it was in the beginning, before the word, in the silence and darkness of a mother's safekeeping.

This is your fate, said the palmist to her eleven-year-old self, you cannot escape it. His eyes glimmered at her like a lighted train on the night horizon.

Will he be a nice man? asked her eleven-year-old self doubtfully, too young for outrage, still open to the possibilities of things. She lifted a strand of her hair, dry and frazzled in the winter morning cold.

He will not, said the palmist, laughing. He will be a tyrant, like the Emperor Aurangzeb, and demand warm socks in the summer and lunch at midnight. He will live without logic or dietary balance.

Enough with such nonsense, Chinoy! Her mother bustled out of the kitchen, flapping a dishrag as if in truce.

She was surprised the palmist knew such details. Less surprised later that this, her mother's black sheep cousin, would soon graze out a fortune in far Minnesota. Someone she had met one summer and would not meet again.

When I marry, said her eleven-year-old self to black sheep uncle Chinoy, there will be a hundred elephants and a prince. I will be a princess and live in a palace made of cake.

Oh, bah! Pooh! said Chinoy.

America-intent palmist-liar, what could he know?

NINA NOW LIVED a few hundred miles northwest of New York City, in a quiet town attended by busy highways as if it were a lull in a conversation. "Everything goes everywhere," she wrote to her mother and sisters in her first week in Ithaca as Siddharth's new wife. "You hop into a car, consult a map, calculate the hours, and you can be anywhere." In the summer they hoped to drive to California. She described America in terms of distances from a lighted center: New York, Los Angeles, Chicago, Washington DC. As if every location she inhabited were a faint nebula, limned into definition by a glowing city.

"I don't know if Nina is happy," sighed her mother, Sushila. "Her letters are so odd, full of precise directions, as if she were a traffic policeman." As if we needed to be whistled to and urged onwards or held up at the crossroads. Silly girl!

"Every marriage is a crapshoot," offered Sushila's bachelor nephew, having heard the phrase used by a Bollywood divorcee in television interviews.

"Don't use bad words," said Nina's mother doubtfully. Really, life was so complicated these days. Words, like children, led secret lives, full of implications beyond their compact, obvious borders. *Crap-shoot. Two hundred miles from New York City.* An *idli* is an *idli* to me, though a spongy rice cake to the US-returned, she thought. I use words to say what I mean.

Nina married Siddharth Vellodi in the calm of a northeastern valley town, Dehradun, after three weeks of courtship, which consisted mainly of lime juice quaffed on the verandah every evening with the entire family weighing in through the living-room curtains. Neighbors dropped by with mithai and recommendations. Uncle Taraporevala and his daughter Nilufer, on the verge of their own odyssey to Detroit. ("Be sure to take warm cardigans. Winter clothing is expensive in the US.") Behind them, Talina and her parents, gentle souls lurking in the doorway, beaming kindness and goodwill. ("Send letters. At least postcards. Remember us.") Mean Mrs. Sharma without her whiny son, Chotu, now far away and starting his life over in Boston. (A small blessing there.) Mrs. Sinha, with Mumsy's very own oversalted recipe for Scottish shortbread, presented with a dismissal. ("Biscuits in America, I hear, are called cookies, and filled with sugar.") And uncles, and aunts, and cousins, and cousins many times removed, and in-laws, and in-laws of in-laws, so many snarled and raining down like confetti, impossible to name and disentangle. But Nina hadn't minded these dizzying intrusions. She wanted to be off, out of the drill of college and family outings to see more family, an outward-to-inward pulse that seemed socially incestuous after years of repetition. Siddharth hadn't minded, either. He rarely minded anything, unless it interfered with numbers on a page. To be a math professor required attention and commitment, and Siddharth had no reason to suspect that marriage might be resistant to rational deduction. He saw, too, that Nina was a friendly and poised young woman from a suitably high caste, and with passable etiquette and sterling academic credentials, two degrees, improbably but impressively in infotech and literature. She would find a job in the computer industry burgeoning outside Ithaca, raise two solid citizens from birth to independence, and golf with him in the golden years. And there was no question that she was pretty, with ivory skin and chiseled features, all looked upon with approval by his mother for the promise of comely grandchildren.

Siddharth did not need three weeks to decide he was to marry Nina.

"Now you are a householder," said his beaming father to Siddharth after the wedding ceremony, while Nina smiled collectedly through layers of jasmine garlands. "Now you must be jovial and always in good spirits! That is the secret of a good marriage. Of course, responsibility is Number One. That you should not forget. Do your duty by your wife and children."

Siddharth was grateful to his father. The last time they had held an extended conversation was eight years ago, just before he left India for graduate school in New York City. At that time his father had reminded him of the importance of Indian culture. If he remembered this through thick and thin, he would not give in to base desires. His father quoted the Bhagavad Gita at length, an exercise effective mostly in its symbolism, because Siddharth's knowledge of Sanskrit remained limited, in his years through elementary school and beyond, to mumbled conjugations and elaborate configurations of the sacred word *Om* on his *Abbey Road* LP. But Siddharth had been grateful for that talk too. He was to use it to recover from a love affair with his thesis adviser's daughter that almost cost him his PhD. But recover he did and returned culture-preserved to Nina on the verandah, sipping his bitter dregs with the bracing lime, not minding his impending nuptials at all.

Palmist-liar Chinoy did not come to the wedding—in fact, never returned to India, having become a prosperous restaurateur in St. Paul. But Nina thought of Chinoy as she slipped the last jasmine garland over Siddharth's neck, her eleven-year-old self suddenly risen and awake. She forgot Chinoy's words but remembered the glimmer in his eyes, the buzz of static in her hair.

After two years in Ithaca, Nina had become Americanized, a sad state of affairs, according to family in Dehradun, because it involved the frequent wearing of denim jeans and skimpy T-shirts, and dinners in which rice was substituted by versions of spaghetti roundly described as pasta. Nina's in-laws had come to stay the second summer, after the marriage had enough time to simmer into routine but when Nina was still breathless with the need to please.

"What it is?" inquired her mother-in-law, peering unfavorably at a scarlet coil of tomatoes and mushy skeins.

"Um," said Nina, uncertain herself.

"That means nothing," said her mother-in-law shortly, wrapping up the matter.

The visit was not a success, and not just because of the food. America itself was not the sparkle and color they had anticipated, but a similar waking up into warm days of nothing in particular, with a drive around town in the evenings after Siddharth returned from the university. Nina's mother-in-law missed her extended family, the dropping by of neighbors with snacks or opinions. When the telephone rang, it was usually a salesperson selling them something. The first time she answered the phone, the mother-in-law was elaborately polite, listening intently to a description of a department store insurance policy she had neither the intention nor the ability to buy.

"Thank you very much," she said at the end of five minutes of uninterrupted information, "but I am only a visitor here."

The salesperson muttered something unintelligible, but clearly unpleasant, and rang off.

"The opposite of outsourcing," said Siddharth. "Now the locals are selling you the goods. Ingrafting."

When the in-laws left after two months, they took with them a whole suitcase full of knickknacks from Walmart.

"We now get everything in India," they sighed. "Here it is twice the price!"

The visit was not a success on any grounds.

"I could get a job," said Nina to Siddharth after their departure. "You have a green card, so we won't be deported."

Siddharth was busy, traveling to conferences everywhere from Davenport, Iowa, to Leningrad or Brussels. He undertook these journeys without particular enthusiasm or complaint, understanding that they were an extension of his work, like committee meetings in the park. The view was better, but the conversation anticipated.

Nina was not invited on the trips, though she yearned to visit Europe, mostly to match her idea of it with the reality to be encountered.

"You'll be bored," Siddharth told her, "with nothing to do while I'm at away the conference. Anyway, wives don't really come along to things like this."

So Nina took up a yoga class at the Y taught by Swami Achudananda, who turned out to be a young, bearded, golden-haired Lutheran now lapsed and refocused. He refused to tell anyone his real name, hiding it under layers of middle-class mystery. She undertook the asanas with a religiosity that would have surprised her parents, who were accustomed to her collection of REM CDs and her book shrine to Agatha Christie. Now both Nina and Swami Achudananda were commemorating India in the Y's newly refurbished high-domed gym that substituted for a basketball court.

"It's another aspect of globalization," said Siddharth, laughing. "The world at the Y. The United Nations of Suburbia."

When Siddharth left for Hilo, Hawaii, in early September, Nina joined the book club that met every Thursday on the second floor of the local library. She wanted to be well balanced in both body and mind, and a quick survey of her recent life had left her convinced that her mind had simply keeled over, flattened by soap operas and boredom. Yoga enriched the body and soul but seemed to leave her reaching for words, something she could paint her experiences with and so discover them anew.

Siddharth had no objection to this new enterprise, or even a comment, Nina was relieved to note.

The library was still air-conditioned, the cooling system left on purposely after the overheated summer. September was June this year, holding its hot breath before the sudden onset of winter. Most people at the library seemed to understand that the season they were in was just a safekeeping of a past insouciance, the sort that sweltering days bring upon you, half-dazed and wandering through the streets.

The book discussion coordinator was Diane Brimm, a retired professor of world literature who now divided her time between reading new fiction and tending her vegetable garden. In winter, it was books entirely. Her reading list tended to the esoteric, with names known only to graduate students of the offbeat variety.

"What ever happened to Hemingway?" demanded the man sitting next to Nina, frowning because it was a joke.

Everybody laughed, all six of the group members, Mary Ann with a toddler, Jake the part-time truck driver, Amos from the Co-op, Zami the dental assistant, Nina, and Daniel himself, though it was his joke. Diane Brimm remained thoughtful.

"Hemingway is everywhere—" she said carefully, and indeed a neighborhood student café was called Hemingway's Hideaway.

That was not quite what she meant, though.

She meant, Nina assumed, that the obvious was passé. The esoteric was good. Globalization, Siddharth might have said, literary outsourcing, your language returned in a new accent, a new idiom, but thank God didn't say, wasn't here to say it.

"—and so we read the different, the challenging. We inhabit new spaces we may never before have imagined."

Her eyes rested briefly on Nina. A wrench in the works. But then she could bring her different perspective to bear upon Coetzee, upon Janet Frame. It could certainly work out, with the right urging.

The first time he invited her out was after the reading group had struggled mightily over French experimental fiction, including Alain Robbe-Grillet's "The Secret Room," which, by consensus after the discussion, was considered an ambush on the part of Diane Brimm, not at all an afternoon's enjoyment.

"It's all description," complained Zami, the dental assistant. "No action or plot. On the floor lies a dead girl covered in blood, a man with a cape looks her over, and the only thing I remember is that they're somewhere next to a spiral staircase."

Diane Brimm closed her eyes briefly and remembered why she was here. To spread great literature, the vast brocade of it, over the sleeping world.

"Permit yourself to see," she said in summary, setting her voluminous Norton Anthology down on the table like an edict, "how the writer paints a portrait of an abiding sadism through the bland stereotypes—the bleeding victimized woman, the skulking criminal. Allow yourself to be immersed in the moment, without prejudice or expectation, so that the scene is at once a stage setting—an unreality—and a truth, a murderous event, an undecipherable loss. See its utter impersonal formality and its human tragedy."

The group shifted uneasily, feeling, and not without merit, that they were attending a graduate seminar for especially unprepared students. Next week's reading was a better collection of stories from Australia—already familiar subject matter, given the new Outback Steakhouse and old Crocodile Dundee movies. The group cheered up a bit and left without rancor.

"This is a two-éclair recovery," he said cheerfully, pushing the plate full of confections toward her in Hemingway's Hideaway Café. His first chin sank into the second one, safely cushioned, cradled.

Nina allowed herself to notice him completely for the first time, though they were four classes into the fall. She took careful note of his expanding girth, his faded blue jeans, his age (fifty? fifty-five?), his even-tempered smile, his partly balding head with a blond ponytail like a comma pausing down his back. A red flannel shirt, open blue eyes, the flop of his paunch over black corduroys. Why didn't they add up to a picture she could remember? How tall was he? Five feet ten?

"What do you do?' she asked him, noticing that despite the offer, there was only one éclair. But two cream puffs. Maybe that was what he meant.

Retired now, he was a self-employed insurance agent, before that a schoolteacher, middle school PE and health. He enjoyed reading poetry, but his passion was inventing things. He had in the works a sleeping bag with the capacity to store heat for up to six hours. Also, a kettle that hooted at boiling point, like an owl. Vietnam gave him these ideas, though the how and why were hard to explain. He was looking for financial backing, but with the economy and the war, no one cared much for such things. He had traveled to China last May with his church committee and was now widening his horizons with tap-dancing lessons on Tuesdays and the reading group meeting on Thursdays. And on her recommendation, possibly yoga on Mondays, if his bad back held up. Other times he was mostly free.

Free to do what? thought Nina. Should she invite him—invite the group—to dinner? Her heart sank at the prospect of summoning up an entire meal. *Whatitis?*

He was unlike the Americans in Siddharth's department, those quiet scholars dreaming in equations. When they addressed her (though infrequently), the scholars spoke in tones of courtly detachment, in diction formal as a tuxedo: "And what portion of the rise in 1960s poverty might you attribute to the first two intractable five-year plans?" or "How does the democratically sanctioned dynastic rule of the Nehrus compare with the ubiquitous political presence here of our very own Kennedy royalty?" But always that slight edge, the winkless knowing. *Ingrafting.*

"It's another aspect of globalization," Nina said wildly to the quizzical faculty, causing Siddharth to raise an eyebrow in embarrassment. *That means nothing.* But it did. Democratic royalty. Now, being here, eating éclairs with a tap-dancing man.

"Tell me," he said, leaning across the table, almost touching her hand and so close she felt his breath on her face. "Will you guys eat beef in India now that McDonald's plans to set up there? Or will they sell seaweed burgers? Pretty gross, hey? That's what I've been thinking."

Nina was charmed by the purposelessness of this encounter. She looked forward to more.

"How's the literary yammering going?" inquired Siddharth. This had been a hard day. His graduate student had flunked his qualifying exam, and by extension the blame was his. Why didn't he get the smarter ones, the penniless and brilliant Chinese or Koreans who were thought to be descending in droves on campuses everywhere? A swarm of low-costs, he said once to Nina, who sat without movement, unperturbed.

"We read Robbe-Grillet," she told him, indifferently, as if such reading were an everyday occurrence.

Siddharth looked suspicious. He read Robbe-Grillet. Also Camus and the early Sartre. A sequence of questions lined up in his head, waiting to be fired, but wisely he desisted, seeing a larger accommodation at stake, a commotion to be stilled in their separate paths.

"Terrific!" he said, resorting to the language of expectation and daily traffic, knowing the patter would help them reach across and reaffirm not a truce, for no war had been called, but a careful and willed neutrality.

They were entering their third year of marriage. The bedroom blinds were lifted in the morning and drawn at night, their eyes opened and shut with similar ritual, the sandalwood incense sticks lit daily, the invocations chanted to gods neither of them believed in, dinners ordered at the cheaper restaurant chains, the expectation of hope.

"Letter from my mother this morning," said Siddharth, tossing an envelope at Nina. "She sent you recipes."

The next Thursday, by the reading group's consensus, was their best-ever fiction discussion. Elizabeth Jolley, what was not to love in her characters, those prickly, muddled losers? Or Colleen McCullough, epic and true. Prose that connected with all of them, straightforward and insightful, not dancing the cancan in feather boas.

"As you notice," said Diane Brimm, gathering up her books, smiling upon her protégés, "the power of literature is in its abundance—of subject, style, intention. As we read, we open our own selves to ourselves, and so we recognize the multitudes within us. That is what great writing does for the reader."

The reading group was never sure how to take Diane Brimm's concluding proclamations but set them down to a retirement sans audience. Nina was especially sympathetic, seeing the Siddharth-to-be in the years ahead, shorn and wobbly as any unsheltered lamb. The thought made her tender and loving as proximity never could, and she ascribed her newfound gentleness to the power of literature, to recognizing her pushing, fussy multitudes.

His name was Daniel Braver.

He had been in the army during the Vietnam War, just a teenager when drafted. There he had seen things he could no longer name. His first real girlfriend was Vietnamese, a concert violinist and a painter of natural landscapes. (He still had one of her watercolors, pink swirls of cherry blossoms in the spring, white mountains in a blooming desert. A beautiful thing.) But a spy for the North, as it turned out. He was lucky not to have been court-martialed. Instead he spent four years in Vietnam and came home decorated. His ponytail was a form of memory, a way of connecting to the past. Nina had begun laughing dutifully over a chocolate cupcake at Hemingway's, thinking this was a joke, when to her distress she realized he had just shared a secret of importance, a personal signifier of sorts. She stopped at once and choked on the cupcake, which changed the subject and the flurry of accompanying actions to the question of her immediate survival, avoiding the whirlpool moment for them both. She learned, too, that he was a pianist with a love for Beethoven, and that he had once played for the county orchestra.

"I'd play for you," he said boldly.

Nina stared at him, puzzled, her hair rising lightly at the nape of her neck. Would he lunch at midnight?

"Have you heard of Aurangzeb?" she asked him.

He had not.

"Do you have children?"

He had two. He was divorced, his wife remarried and in New Mexico. He saw his children rarely. They were adults now, so not strictly children. They called him Dan the Weirdo Man in their infrequent letters. He took it as a sign of their affection.

"You eat too many sweets," she said to him, eyeing the four cupcake wrappers on his plate. "You need dietary balance."

Nina realized that she was speaking out of sheer fright and resolved not to visit Hemingway's Café with Daniel anymore. She would excuse herself after the book discussion and go straight home. All her multitudes would have to be pushed back into the bottle and the top screwed on tight. One person was enough to deal with.

"I have to go now," she said, and left him alone with a coffee cup and the wrappers, surrounded by young people boisterously out of class, their whooping encircling his table in mad streamers of noise.

Nina took the home pregnancy test at four o'clock the next afternoon. A thin blue line showed up clearly, rising out of nowhere like an automatic fence. Leaning against the bathtub, Nina held up the tester to the light, her left hand resting against her stomach. Outside, the early autumn leaves were burning into their fireworks colors, reds and orange, burnished gold. She saw the blue sky through their brilliant foliage, streaks of sobriety through the celebration. She would rejoice and be still. This changes everything, she thought.

Dear Mummy, I have good news for you. . . .

Three weeks later Sushila in Dehradun wept with joy. Policeman or not, Americanized with brusque directions or not, her daughter knew her priorities, her family duties. Sushila would make plans now for an extended trip to the US, for who else would take care of her daughter at this important time? Certainly not the in-laws. "We were given some cold strands with tomato sauce," Mrs. Vellodi had said, looking injured. "But I have sent her recipes, so Siddharth can be assured of good Indian meals. Of course, that is only a joke. We love her like a daughter."

She skipped the next Thursday, which was to have been a discussion on V. S. Naipaul's *A House for Mr. Biswas*, partly because Diane Brimm had said to the group the earlier Thursday, waving at Nina in an unequivocal sort of way: "We have our own cultural expert here to provide us with an insider's perspective." Diane Brimm's sudden abdication of responsibility made Nina nervous, never having been to Trinidad herself, and vaguely offended that Naipaul's ancestral provenance seemed to imply that the two of them were somehow kin. No one suggested that Diane Brimm was Janet Frame's country cousin simply because they might both have, at some far reach in time, come from Liverpool or Sheffield or Yorkshire. But the real reason was that Nina wanted time now to herself, to weigh and parse the future days, to set timetables and limits for the coming of the life to be. She cleaned and cooked and arranged and scrubbed, a dervish with a duster and a mop. She was brutally efficient in her intentions, taut and grim with joy. Nesting, said her obstetrician, after the first quick checkup.

The telephone rang several times that morning. Nina ignored it, disconcerted that no one left a message.

"I think you're finally settling down," observed Siddharth, disbelieving. "Sometimes it takes us off-the-boaters a while. You're coming through."

The Friday after the missed Naipaul discussion was when she first saw him, at the local grocer's while she was inspecting organic carrots for a salad. Daniel waved to her. She waved back.

The next time was on Saturday at the dry cleaners. He had a coat to clean, no surprise there, what with winter coming on.

On Monday he was at the dentist's, reading *People* magazine.

Later in the evening, he was at the Y, talking earnestly to Swami Achudananda. He was planning on taking up yoga, after all. Or had he said not?

On Tuesday, she felt an odd thrumming inside her chest like an electric wire as she watched him drive by their tidy brown ranch house, and then up the street again, and then down again.

When Siddharth returned from work on Wednesday, she gathered up her courage, not so much from fear as from the sense of impending ridicule to follow.

"There's a man who keeps following me," she said. "He's a vet from my reading group."

"A vet?" asked Siddharth, puzzled. "Do we have pets?"

"A Vietnam vet," said Nina, the thrumming in her heart mixed now with confusion. "He told me he was in the war. I think he's been following me for about a week."

"Tell him to go away." Siddharth had papers to grade. "Tell him you're married and not interested. Or are you?"

"Stop it," said Nina. "This isn't funny."

"I'm not saying it is," said Siddharth patiently. One had to draw a line. "But did you encourage him in any way? Did you talk a lot to him?"

"We drank coffee after the reading group meetings." Not possible now to mention the éclairs and cream puffs—a doorway to a joke.

"There you are, then," said Siddharth, as if solving a self-evident equation. "You need to be more aware of your actions, Nina. You can't just go on dates with strange men and not feel you're encouraging them. I'm not saying this is your fault, but you have to understand what you do. Would I go out with a woman not my wife? It sends a message."

"You don't understand," said Nina. "We were just talking. They weren't dates. You could go out with any woman you want—I wouldn't think anything of it. We talked about books and the group and our lives. Do listen and stop judging. I'm really scared."

Siddharth sighed, irritated.

"We'll call the police," he suggested, "if he's around you again? Give it a couple of days. My guess is he'll go away, find another—" He hesitated, thinking. "Friend."

Nina noted the hesitation, noted Siddharth's gathering up of books and his abrupt closing of the den door. She was the unfunny joke, and for just a moment she felt triumphant, like an athlete on the floor, scraped and winded but still across the finish line.

Over the next few days, she stayed home. A message on her machine from Diane Brimm said: "Nina! Where are you? We were so looking forward to your views on *Biswas*—but never mind! Next week we begin our journey into Latin versions of magical realism. I know that you, with your inventive mind, will love it. Call me for the reading list. I'm home after six."

Two other messages were blank—a silence, then a click. Nina erased those messages immediately, as if waving a wand to wipe them out of memory. Magical realism for the moment. She did not call Diane Brimm.

She knew she would meet him again, so it was no surprise to see Daniel the next morning outside her kitchen window, a fixture like a mailbox at the curb. He stood next to a bush, half hidden by the foliage, and Nina was momentarily distracted by an odd snuffling noise from somewhere around his stomach, until she realized he was clutching a small brown thing—a purse? A dog? A dog, a pug. A wrinkled, wheezing pug.

She drew aside the curtain and said firmly, "I can see you."

Daniel moved out of the bushes and held out the dog. "This is Pascal," he said. Then he walked out onto the street and turned the bend.

On his return in the afternoon, he was all shy and sweet, a bride at the altar with a nosegay in which he kept his face hidden. Except the nosegay was the pug, so decrepit and smelling faintly of mothballs, it could well have been stuffed. She invited him in. There was no other way out.

"This is my baby," Daniel explained to Nina, lifting his nose into the clean air. "He's fourteen. He has fleas in the summer, but by winter they're gone."

Nina decided to take the no-nonsense approach, all her traffic policeman talents swirling into the vortex of this one moment.

"I think you've been telephoning me and not answering when I pick up. I think you've been following me," she said, not adding, Of course you have. That's why you're here. "You need to stop doing this. It's really not very pleasant."

"In the winter, he wears a tartan coat. Everyone says to me, is that a dog or a doll? A grown man with a doll. I don't like that." He waited for a response and, when none was forthcoming, offered himself stage directions. "I'll sit down, then," and he did so very gingerly at the table, as if the chair was hot.

"Easy now," he said.

Nina heard the whine of a neighbor's leaf blower, the everyday-ness of her life caught somewhere outside her being, spinning out its insistent and bland routines. She looked around her dining room for a thing to hold on to, something familiar and known.

Her eye fell on the lazy Susan with its empty center.

"That's real pretty," remarked Daniel, appreciatively. "When the kids were little, we hid candy in there, so the kids couldn't find it. My wife and I, we loved M&M's. The kids had bad teeth, so we were doing them a favor."

"What's her name?" asked Nina.

"Margarita," said Daniel. "Like the drink. I called her Maggie. Maggie and Pascal are my loves."

He began emptying his pockets, laying the contents on the table. A fork, a roll of cinnamon mints, a scrap of paper with a grocery list, an open penknife, a flat aluminum key. He set them out horizontally, arranging by size, in descending order. The fork, the paper, the knife, the mints, the key.

"This is my life now," he said, with a debutante-like nonchalance.

Pascal lay quietly by his feet, wheezing.

"What do you want from me?" asked Nina, feeling, and not without reason, that she was in a poorly made film with silly actors. Caught like a fly in amber, if not for the leaf blower with its busy beckoning, its unlikely keening grace.

"I have a present for you," said Daniel, "but you never stop to take it. You're always rushing, rushing. You waved to me just once, in the grocery store. I'm not dirt, you know, I'm human."

"I'm sorry," said Nina, feeling the old thrumming return, sending the policeman packing. "I'm going to have a baby."

"Well, now," said Daniel. "What does your husband say?"

"I haven't told him," said Nina.

Daniel pursed his lips. "You're not that happy, then," he said. "You're just another liar."

Pascal was getting bored. He began sneezing plaintively, sneezing and wheezing like some obscure musical instrument from the Middle Ages.

"In Vietnam," said Daniel, settling his first chin snugly into the second, "there's a story about a secret race of women, solitary members of a ghost world. They breed without the need for men and live under the earth, appearing for only twenty-four hours at harvest time. Then they plow through miles of paddy fields, destroying the rice crops with a puff of breath, killing elephants with a single glance. Late at night they rest, covered in leaves warmed by the heat of the sun for six entire hours—sleeping bags, I like to say, given by nature—till the hooting of owls wakes them up in the early morning and draws them onward, step by step. Men are afraid of their power. Scientists have studied their story and found it to be true. My information is based on experience as well. I have met such women in Vietnam. They saved me from shrapnel in the ditches. They gave me shelter in their bed of leaves. I have to tell you this in case you get lost. There is always a hooting owl to guide you through. Remember this." Daniel ran his finger carefully over his chins, back and forth, as if testing for stubble or further insights. Abruptly he leaned closer into Nina, checking first over his shoulder for eavesdroppers. "But in the spring, their heads fill with nightmares of white fangs and blooming deserts. With metal rain, gunpowder in the petals. Then they rage and kill in utter darkness. In the spring you must avoid these women. They must not be touched."

"You're storytelling," said Nina, after a pause. "I don't believe you. I think you're lying. I don't know if you were in Vietnam. I'm not even sure about Margarita." There was no doubt now that he was completely batty, but a Pascalian battiness, all coughed up and battle-weary. He was the one covered in blood, she had become the caped villain. Her heart resented this surprise, but she felt her fear subside, the lowering of a water level on a hot, hot day, a loss to underscore the broken land.

Daniel stood up, lurching gently against the brittle air. "I must go now," he said. "I won't overstay my welcome. But I have a present for you." He gathered up his belongings, leaving the penknife in the middle of the table like a silver fish, a thing out of its element, bare and prone.

Through the window, Nina watched him walk down the street, and waved when he turned the corner. He was only human. But Daniel did not look back.

It was not the hooting of owls she remembered, but these: a dry winter day, a palmist's sly laugh, a foretelling of children, a spiral staircase, two cream puffs, the multitudes within, a clean silver blade. When her daughter was born one quiet spring morning, Nina leaned into the child's crumpled face and traced out the baby's soft features with her fingers. Pressing her body against this new canvas, she felt like a painter or a blind woman—as if no matter how varied the colors or uncertain the terrain, her weight equaled a promise of keeping, a thing to hold on to, a shape remembered and known.

The Bonny Hills of Scotland

MRS. SINHA PUT one in mind of claws and bone. With a personality as angular and brittle as her frame, she was scarcely the kind of woman to inspire love. Still, we hoped that her character was not entirely without its merits. She would, for example, carefully turn off the lamps before leaving a room and was most attentive to cats. Frugality and compassion for the dumb, said mother, stretching the truth into glowing virtue. But no matter how we attempted to gloss over her flaws, Mrs. Sinha remained tall and resolute in her unloveableness. As she put it, she hated waste and cats didn't talk back. That summed up Mrs. Sinha's philosophy of life and set us to repositioning our gentler interpretations of her motives. With her we were always teetering on that bridge between sympathy and censure, swinging whichever way the moment took us. Mrs. Sinha never abetted our companionable efforts, though she often swung us right off the bridge into offended silence. This was one of those times.

It was unseasonably cool that afternoon in March, the air flirting with the frost as it fizzled and disappeared in the grass. Our house was calm, free of thieving uncles and policemen, and life had settled into routine. At the foothills of the Himalayas, the Siwalik Hills dreamed into their blue haze, pine needles clattering like stones into the gullies. One of those days when life moves by slowly, trundling across time like an old cart. Today on my eighth birthday, I would hoist balloons and ritually down fennel-flavored yellow cake from the HolyWood Bakery, a name suggesting cinematic aspirations or a gastro-religious conundrum. Most important, I would test my adult future in my new red high-heeled sandals.

I sat on the embankment outside our house and watched the clouds waft by, shaping and reshaping themselves as they covered and parted the sky. There was a world ahead of me unformed and waiting, and I felt this knowledge descend on me like sunlight, warm and encompassing but intangible. I sat with the strange feeling that I was synonymous with everything around me, as if we were all contained within one word, the trees, the clouds, the clattering pines, and myself in a knit dress and red sandals. We were all sustained within this sweep, a pure note in a melody. I was thinking to myself that this was the best birthday present, nothing given or taken but simply there, when my reverie was crossed by a big black umbrella brandished furiously at the foot of the embankment.

Attached to one end of the umbrella was an agitated Mrs. Sinha. Dressed in a pink sari, she complemented the quiet azure sartorially if not in spirit. Her thin body, all elongated possibility, had sharpened into spikes, jabbing the air as she made small lunging movements toward me. Then she gathered her breath into a single climactic blast.

"Wretched girl!" she roared. "Bring back Queen Victoria!"

I struggled up, indignant.

Swung off the bridge again.

Queen Victoria was a particularly unpleasant feline, one of eighteen in Mrs. Sinha's home, who was partial to vicious attacks on assorted socks and large dogs. Her attitude to me was little better, except that she was more metaphoric in her hatred, preferring elaborate arrangements of hisses and narrowed eyes to actual combat. In retaliation, I threw anything of aerodynamic proportions at Queen Victoria, who was usually satisfyingly if only momentarily terrorized. Mrs. Sinha, having taken note of our exchanges through her bedroom window, now put her sentiments into succinct terms.

"If you have my cat," she said, "I'll smack your little face."

As I saw it, the statement left no room for ambiguity.

"It's my birthday, Auntie," I said to Mrs. Sinha, hoping to soften her up. "Would you like some cake?"

Mrs. Sinha froze into solid rock before shooting out an ultimatum in a hail of razor-edged pebbles.

"Get that cat back," she hissed, "or I'll birthday you!"

Then she waved her umbrella triumphantly at the sky and stamped up to her house.

It seemed without question that Mrs. Sinha had no need to be loved. Married to Brijesh Sinha, an army colonel killed in Burma in World War II, she had lived all her eighty years in an ivy-and-rose-covered cottage, Mountain Rest, her home under the canopy of the Himalayas. A remnant of the colonial Raj, she still referred to "darling Mumsy" famed in the 1930s for the elegant teas she arranged for British officers' wives at the Doon Club. During these soirees, Mumsy played the piano and Mrs. Sinha (then plain Leelavati Sen) accompanied her with rousing ditties celebrating the bonny hills of Scotland. These days she sang alone, though her voice could carry over the roofs of three houses.

Oh, I am come to the low countrie
Och on, och on, och rie!
Without a penny in my purse,
To buy a meal to me.
It was na sae in the Highland hills,
Och on, och on, och rie!
Nae woman in the country wide
Sae happy was as me.

My guess was that Mrs. Sinha had never so much as seen a bonny hill, but that didn't matter, she was sae happy anyway with all things haggis and tartan. Children like me who ran barefoot and ate chapatis and pickles with lip-smacking relish Mrs. Sinha considered only marginally civilized. To her, Indian Independence was merely an annoyance, the kind one politely ignored as if it were a spot on an evening dress, and she still spoke of the departed British presence in India with a nostalgia reserved for first loves.

To compensate for their absence, she sent her only son, Parashar, aka Bunty, to England, where he took root and flowered into a pompous accent and tailored clothes. A tall and perpetually bent man, he put us in mind of wilting shrubbery. With each yearly visit home, he wilted further, until I felt there would be a time when he was completely horizontal and inert.

Nonetheless, he brought life to Mrs. Sinha, who blazed all the lights on recklessly when he arrived and switched them off entirely when he left. No frugality there. Yet I never saw them exchange a fond word. They simply sat across from each other in their living room horsehair chairs, sipping tea morning and evening, while visitors like my family gazed hopefully at the clock for reprieve from our fifteen-minute social calls.

And when Bunty left for England at the end of each summer, fashionably elongating his sibilants, "Sss see you sssoon! Goodbye! Tootles!" in tones of modulated boredom to friends and foes alike, Mrs. Sinha always said mysteriously, "Well, that's done," as if Bunty were a well-risen cake. Then she fed her cats severely, now temporarily demoted to mewling aberrations in her life of composed ritual. After that, through the rest of the year, her house was always dark at night, except for a lone lamp at the window like a beam calling ships home. She had a daughter, too—at least was rumored to have had one—who long ago set off for America in an orange sari and was never heard of again. Maya Sinha, or more commonly Bunny, she of the reputed tossing curls and cigarette holder. When my mother once encroached upon this guarded territory while exchanging notes with Mrs. Sinha on various methods of polishing my base potential into a shining diamond, Mrs. Sinha merely said, "Daughters are such a bother." And the subject was not broached again.

From the corner of my eye, I saw Mrs. Sinha about to enter her house. She lived next door to us, so monitoring her creative exits and entrances didn't require particular detective acumen. Mrs. Sinha was well aware of her audience and played to it with unfiltered self-regard. Tossing her head back dramatically, she hummed Scottish ballads to make clear to the hoi polloi that she was a woman of cultured upbringing. Or, when it was raining, she picked up her sari skirts and grimly, nimbly, negotiated puddles with ballerina precision to indicate she had both grace and pluck. The variations on her comings and goings were many, geared to inspire the common herds. Today, though, was umbrella-twirling day. Wheeling around just before she entered her front door, Mrs. Sinha spun her umbrella my way ominously, bellowing, "Queen Victoria! In an hour or less! Silly, silly girl!" Then she swept indoors and banged the door shut, her work done.

I closed my eyes, mainly to punish Mrs. Sinha by imagining her in purple pantaloons and galoshes, but dozed off unexpectedly for perhaps half an hour, bathing my drowsy senses in the lacquer-cool afternoon. In the trees the mynahs rustled, squabbling over resting places. The postman, weary from his climb through the old British cantonment roads, trudged woodenly uphill, a clockwork soldier, expecting, as usual, to be bawled out by Mrs. Sinha for his indolence. Out beyond in the valley, smoke rose from the villagers' huts. A small train bound for the plains tooted merrily in the foothills—from my vantage point, a toy in the world of make-believe where I slept like Gulliver.

I dreamed, as I fell into this numbing sleep, of ships with umbrella mastheads. Bright green and gold, scarlet and purple, they were the colors of wedding saris, their sterns zari-bright. I stood at the helm of one of these ships—but whether I guided the ship or whether it guided me I couldn't tell. Instead, all I felt was the lift and dip of the waves beneath me, taking me inexorably toward a horizon so gray with clouds it seemed a stretch of bleak canvas. The heft and fall of the waves made a swishing sound that phrased itself into a song, the way the wheels of a train seem to chuff into words. I listened carefully. "Smack-yoface smack-yoface," sang the ship.

"That's not very nice," I said loftily. "No balloons or cake for you today."

The ship rose high, as if insulted, and for a moment I thought I might touch the gray clouds, so close were we to the sky. Then with no warning the horizon split neatly into two, and the ship sailed on— but without me. Now I stood on land, in ribbons and bows, balloons in hand, shod in red sandals, while the ship in full umbrella-flight shattered into light as it fell into the broken skyline.

"See you next year!" I called. "See you. See you!"

Mee—ow. A baleful marble met my gaze. Two marbles. Cold, hard, green. I sat up groggily and there she was: Queen Victoria. Fat and lofty, a regal tub, she studied me with the enthusiasm of royalty for a minion. Her paw outstretched, she made a fine red line down my arm, then settled back to admire her filigree work.

"I'll birthday you!" I said grimly to Queen Victoria, tucking her safely under an arm. She slumped immediately into a meek and shapeless ball, but I wasn't taking any chances—especially since the marbles were rolling wildly, testing for the right pause.

Marching purposefully to Mrs. Sinha's door, I rehearsed the big moment. There would be cries of surprise and welcome. Perhaps there'd be an abject apology and pleas to stay to tea. This was to be countered with the dismissal "Oh no, I must go home for cake." It would be clear who had class. Elongated sibilants, pooh.

I rang the doorbell. Thoughts rushed through my head. *Holy-Wood cake. Holy woodcake. Ho li woo cake. Chinese food. Rhyming nonsense very good.*

I rang the bell again, then pushed open the door.

Mrs. Sinha was in her armchair, a letter folded neatly in her lap. A grandfather clock overhead looked sternly down at me, seeming to chide an indiscretion. Several fat cats, collapsed with lunch, dotted the floor.

Mrs. Sinha seemed to think I was someone else. "It's all right, Mumsy," she said. "Really, quite all right."

I cleared my throat. "It's me," I said. "I found the cat."

Mrs. Sinha looked dreamily into the grate as if the ashes were about to rise and make a fire.

"The cat," I said uncertainly.

She saw me for the first time.

"Stay to tea," she said, an imperative issued in the tone of an army command, but what kept me there was a something in the movement of Mrs. Sinha's fingers, restless like Queen Victoria but an agitation without bite.

We sat across from each other in the punishing horsehair chairs. Queen Victoria, fortified by a saucer of milk, settled moodily by the grate, eyeing me with a malevolent familiarity, waiting for a false move.

A silence followed, during which interlude Mrs. Sinha stared at me intently.

"You're quite unwashed," she said finally. "Who let you in?"

"I'm Anu," I said. "My name is Anu. From next door." I swatted a hand vigorously in the general direction of next door.

Mrs. Sinha looked alarmed. "Are there mosquitoes?" she said.

There was another pause.

"He's gone," said Mrs. Sinha.

Who? I made a noise somewhere between a cough and an interrogative.

Mrs. Sinha offered me the letter as if it were cake, and I accepted it politely and read of Bunty's death in a car accident on those bonny hills that weren't home anymore. The note from the London solicitors was brief, printed under a flourish of oversized black letters: *Bronwen, Smith and Brown.*

The numbers on the clock seemed to dance, turning and twisting time, making the past the present, overturning the future. The room seemed different, filled with crinolines and handfans held by British dowagers, smiling brittle women whose faces were rotting, their white powder and paint flaking off like leprosy. And the clock tick-tocked in a kind of wretched gargling, the throaty rattle of dying men. Voices, like summer parasols, rose and fell, twirling giddily or folding into whispers. In the cacophony of sound and images, Mrs. Sinha's fingers drummed a safe return. I read the note twice and tried to find something to say.

But Mrs. Sinha would have none of it. She had risen, striding grimly into the next room, and then into the next and then the next. It struck me that she was switching on all the lamps, filling the bright afternoon with a light that couldn't show. I was in her dream now, a photograph negative in her shattered blaze. A horizon opened up before me, a far line where her purple pantaloons and my smart mouth did an unlikely two-step and collided. I stood watching her, and all I could think was that this was my birthday, now both given and taken, and as I remembered this, I thought of the magic word that seemed to hold all things in joy. If I knew what it was, I would give it to her, unlock the afternoon into transparency. But for Mrs. Sinha, marching through the day, words were fierce artillery, stout umbrellas pointed high.

"Go away," she barked. "Ssssilly girl."

Lounging by the grate, Queen Victoria looked up briefly, buffing her paws with a pink tongue. Then, rich with milk, she yawned and fell asleep.

As it turned out, I was the one who needed saving. Mrs. Sinha lived on for another twenty-three years, more infuriated by the minute and negotiating puddles and the changing landscape of India with her unfailing dexterity. In her last decades, the Congress Party lost its monopoly, religious uprisings roared up and then sputtered, political parties grew and splintered, the economic markets opened, radio was elbowed aside by a television boom in which *Dallas* reruns became as common as advertisements for Binaca toothpaste. But at the foothills of the Himalayas, halfway up a small hill, a woman sat unshaken by the swirl around her, counting her days by the perfidiously slow gait of the postman, the late running of the mountain train. Her newspapers still came from England, some two weeks late, and she squinted at the shenanigans of the royal family and the rise and fall of the Conservative Party with the same reproachful attention. My mother's letters always included Mrs. Sinha in a postscript. How nice it was that Leela was taking a walk these days. What a pity her maid had run off with Mrs. Chopra's gardener. A shame she had had a fall in the bathroom, but nothing to worry about, the guardrail on the tub was her saving grace. Her death from a sudden heart attack at 103 was a release, said my mother, for who would want to spend her last days on a bed, staring at the ceiling, waiting for nobody?

But a somebody who turned up after a week was Bunny Sinha, the long-lost daughter I'd once relegated to legend. A very nice girl, wrote my mother approvingly in even, flowing penmanship, though Bunny must have been as old as she was, perhaps older. A very nice girl who took care of things, sold the house, spoke in complete sentences to the neighbors, without hissing, and dressed just like any other hometown girl in shalwars and saris. No blue jeans here, wrote my mother meaningfully, such a Nice Indian Girl despite a lifetime in America.

This was the first I'd heard of it.

An address followed. Bunny would love to see you, wrote my mother, ever the optimist. She lives in Pennsylvania, right next to where you are, on the East Coast.

I live in New Jersey, so the language of approximation was open to debate. According to my mother, anything not California was east of California and thereby close to the East Coast.

Fine, I said to my mother. My sister Nina was in South Bend, and I'd long been planning a drive there. A Pennsylvania stopover en route wasn't impossible.

In truth I had no desire to visit Bunny, who, in fairness, probably had even less interest in me. But one rainy day, a month after my mother's directive, I was talking to a man in a line at the DMV when he said, out of the blue, "How come you guys don't eat beef but like monkey brains?" Just like that, out of nowhere, though we had been discussing the length of the wait before we got to the top of the line, and the way the local school taxes were killing ordinary folk. Turned out, he'd seen *Indiana Jones and the Temple of Doom* more than a dozen times, and planned on watching it again.

For what reason is hard to pinpoint, but I said to him, "If Mrs. Sinha were here, she'd birthday you." And that pretty much put an end to the conversation, though it got me thinking of umbrellas and my past.

Out of stupid homesickness and pique, I went home and dialed Bunny's number, introduced myself, and waited for the brush-off.

"Do come to visit," said Bunny, "whenever you're in the neighborhood."

Her voice was soft and modulated, a contrast to Mrs. Sinha's power blast but exactly like the legions of boarding-school girls who had passed through the hands of desperately English Anglo-Indian teachers over fifty years ago, sheltered in their very own ersatz England in the mountains. I listened in vain for an American inflection. There was none. Such a Nice Girl. Despite a lifetime in America, she was possibly the last Brit in India.

What a coincidence, I said, I was just on my way to visit my sister Nina in Indiana and could swing by central Pennsylvania on my way there. Unless, of course, she was busy.

I had the summer off from teaching political science at Rutgers, and my companion of three years, Steven, had gone off on an Alaskan cruise to find himself, or more accurately to lose me (an unenthusiastic lover, as he put it), so there was nothing holding me back. I shut my apartment door with the kind of excitement I'd felt before leaving India for graduate school, but this time the high was tempered with uncharitable skepticism, the curling at the corners that helps wrap around a potential rebuff, a salve in waiting. What if Bunny were an axe murderer, a keeper of chained bears, an international spy? This despite being told by my mother that Bunny had had a long and uninterrupted career as a professor of biology at a liberal arts college in

New England—and, I supposed, was now retired and gardening safely in a Pennsylvania hamlet, dressed in Amish robes. Or at least garbed in something other than an orange sari.

The drive to the heart of Pennsylvania was hot and sticky, a description more palatable when applied to a doughnut. Less than halfway there, I was already regretting the folly of such a decision, this long journey to see a myth made flesh because of an idiot in a license bureau. I stopped at three McDonald's on the way to review my recent past, my peripatetic Steven, my papers newly graded—with my limpet-like Dockers no doubt exacerbating the general discomfort. Go back, go home. Silly, silly girl. Get larger pants. Get a life.

"I see you have no cats!" I said to Bunny brightly, before realizing that Victoria and her ilk were probably long gone anyway, preceding Bunny's arrival at Mountain Rest. Now what could this observation mean? Bunny seemed not to notice, all that excellent breeding from a tony boarding school.

"No cats," she said. "No dogs. No horses. No anyone. Just me."

All around, as we spoke, the hilly Pennsylvania landscape rose and fell, a lift and dip of smooth green waves. The Siwaliks without conifers.

Bunny looked to be in her late sixties. Only my mother could have seen the girl in her. Very thin and tall, she stood about six feet five, a giant by standards for Indian women. Her face, though it took some effort to decipher from my considerably nether view, was a sequence of angularity, a Sinha legacy, though in her case infinitely muted—a sharp, middle-sized nose, slightly sunken cheeks, razor-thin eyebrows, eyes brown and alert as a child's. She wore a suburban uniform of khakis and a loose white shirt, both of which hung from her frame in folds, revealing streaks of parchment yellow skin. I began to see Bunny's need for flight, this stark migrating crane, a quest for a life unlimited by the neighborhood's murmured consolations. *Ohsotall! Ohtootall! Who will marry this poor girl?!*

The house, a white square of siding with green shutters and two bay windows, overlooked a golf course. A few late putting enthusiasts dotted the horizon, bent in commas against the sky. Otherwise the place was still. We walked past the lawn, reaching the back garden with its light-filtered sunroom. Miniature potted roses filled the corners, so many and so blowsy, they seemed almost an infestation. Bunny motioned me to sit on her freshly painted white wicker chairs, and I realized that in its picture-perfect order, this was a house without children. We sat primly, each readying to play our hand, though it was evident we hadn't quite understood the game.

"They grow like weeds," she sighed, reaching out to pick a rose and handing it to me. The moment offered us a distraction, a pastoral pause from the more oiled cycles of small talk, the weather, the price of gasoline, a rising allergy season. The rose lay soft in my cupped palms, a nest of petals. If you cradled it just right, the thorns felt as harmless as a sleeping baby porcupine, meek and tender. *She loves me, she loves me not.* Beyond us on the stoop was a white stone birdbath, thin brown lines cracking across the rim in a zigzag of dazed geography. Beside it, a pot of white daylilies. And on the lawn, between elm trees, a hammock paralyzed in the still evening air. Over the hammock, a last bee keening before it dropped. If not for the yellow down of pollen covering everything around us, we were almost an advertisement for world peace or outdoor furniture.

After the opening pleasantries—the relief of sunshine after this punishing winter, the long drive (and was I hungry?), the problems with her old roof and the need for repairs—we settled into a lull oddly comfortable for two strangers.

"I wanted to see you," said Bunny, "because your mother was so very kind to me. Do you know she sent me dinner every one of those days I was at Mountain Rest, because she felt I had enough on my hands? I thought the gesture was so kind—as much in concern for my mother as for me. Your mother's care touched me deeply."

"Oh." I was embarrassed. I had thought this woman might be an axe murderer, told her I was traveling to South Bend, but she had eaten my mother's chapatis, dusted the gargling grandfather clock, swept the bedrooms, arranged papers, sold real estate, and fallen asleep, probably, in the same old horsehair chair where I once read a letter.

"I'm not much like my mother." It was hard to hold Bunny's gaze even sitting across from her, so far up from my five-foot frame was she. Addressed to her clavicle, the statement sounded evasive. But any higher and my neck would crick.

There was less to say than we had thought, so Bunny played the piano for me, a rousing Mozart, a child's recital in reverse, and we went into her kitchen to a brief recess with black coffee and salty homemade Scottish shortbread. "In America," she said regretfully, "shortbread is a sugar cookie. So much sugar in everything."

We commiserated over lost gastronomic opportunities. I thought of the HolyWood Bakery and my favorite fennel-flavored yellow cake. A black umbrella stuck out of it. I shifted hastily from this unappetizing memory.

With time to fill, or, more accurately, to invest—we leafed through old black-and-white photographs, hoping to establish a place to reach into and draw out from, something to return to in the days ahead as an impetus to a phone call, a New Year's greeting card, or at the very least a tossed-off email. But *What a nice time we had!—a stirring sonata—such fragrant java!—I still think of the* . . . didn't seem enough. Her photographs were sepia-toned, washing the pictures in a sleepy melancholy. Here were Bunny and Bunty riding horses down a leafy gully slippery with stones. Bunny and Mrs. Sinha at the Taj Mahal. Two bonneted infants perched on Colonel Sinha in a lawn chair outside Mountain Rest. Bunty and Mrs. Sinha under a large umbrella, both squinting, displeased by the patchy rain. A photograph of a long, thin British army officer, stern and gimlet-eyed. Even the hazy sepia he glared out of failed to dilute his fury.

"Oof," I said, impressed.

"My father," said Bunny matter-of-factly. "He left for England soon after I was born. We never saw him again." In his place, then, Colonel Sinha, the fond substitute, squatting behind a little girl pointing at the camera. Meek and tender, incapable of harm, she squirmed and smiled, a grafted English rose. The Sinhas' wedding photograph, out of focus. No such photograph of plain Leelavati Sen with the long, thin British officer. No record of his being, none at all.

A later photograph, in vivid color, of a handsome, bearded African American man in a dashiki and a pouf of wavy hair. In his hand a placard with notations now too blurred to read. Another of Mrs. Sinha's secrets?

"Oliver," said Bunny amiably. "We are divorced now. We met in Selma. We were married for ten years."

I thought of Mrs. Sinha, in her hostile chairs, reading the *London Times*, sharing tea with Mumsy, in perpetual waiting for her gimlet-eyed knight, scornful of things not commended by the Queen. Daughters were such a bother. Mrs. Sinha, now asleep in crinolines and silk. But here were Oliver and Bunny waving placards at passing cars, ridiculous and free in flowing scarves and tie-dye robes, so many years ago, so young themselves. And over it all, Bunty in a shattered blaze, Saville Row–suited, hissing impeccably, the shining one in ashes.

"I'd like to see you before I go," I said. "I haven't had a look at you at all."

Now three hours later, Bunny stood up, towering over me, a totem pole protecting a twig, steady but unnecessary. "If you don't mind, that is."

The stone birdbath was about a foot off the ground, and it took one jump to clamber up onto it, to hold out an arm, steady myself against her weight. Our eyes were finally level, my ankles at her knees. I flailed, my feet seesawing on the birdbath that threatened at any moment to collapse, and I clutched at her shoulder, thinking this was my chance to recall her on some later day, out here in the late afternoon light crisscrossed by shadows flat and dull. From up so close, her skin looked different, a fine maze of wrinkles like crushed linen. Her nose seemed longer, now as sharp as Mrs. Sinha's. Her deep-set eyes shone luminous, laser points in a night sky. But on her left cheek was a small brown scar, a brushstroke left by a twig, a fingernail, something temporary and immediate. Unlike the rest of her, it carried no far history. This was a different Bunny for me to photograph in my mind's eye, a negative brightened to wash out the sepia silliness, the planned escapes and willed negotiations that had dimmed and stalled our many lives. We were, to ourselves and to each other, such known and complete strangers.

I held on to her in a daze, disturbing her composure.

She stumbled momentarily, grasped me firmly back, a responsible class monitor ensuring that every student stayed in line.

Bunny's forehead furrowed slightly. "Are you all right, dear?" she said. "You don't look well."

I grabbed at her band of feathered curls to avoid keeling off the birdbath altogether.

Her hair shifted, and then rested lopsided against her head, a jaunty cap.

"Oh my!" said Bunny, breathless, clutching at her wig while steadying my wobbling on the birdbath with her other arm. "Now we're both absurd."

But here we were, the others gone. Steven Alaska-cruising, unlikely to return, Mrs. Sinha dispersed into the ether, my mother cooking breakfast in a distant time zone, our homes in America clean with aerosols and absence. And soon the rooms laid out like waiting hearses, nightgowns neat on covered beds, the televisions mute, the lamps unlit. The hush of dusk, pollen-dusted, shorn of bees.

"I'm not well," I told Bunny convivially, patting her hair back into place, sensing on some receding ship a birthday moment of composure, a memory that forgot its name. Somehow, somewhere, our stories looped together, tied a clean, forgiving knot. Shivers clattered down my back. There might be method to this madness. "I am not entirely well. But then again, I'm all right. I think I might be fine. In fact, clearly on the upswing."

We teetered, planed together, giggling like mad schoolgirls, when I felt bloom in my closed hand her gifted rose—this stab of pain, this crest of blood, a wound welling like a breath.

Almost Theides

MAYA HAS NEVER known anyone who died. Not a grandparent or a rickety neighbor or anyone struck by what Maya's tight-lipped mother Nina referred to (after six months of her own successful chemotherapy) as "the C-word." Maya's mother had brushed aside death as if it were a mosquito and marched forward into a robust if uncharted future.

"Some things need tablets and pills," she announced to Maya, believing a firm explanation fortified the spirit. "Some things just need a strong will."

Maya's mother waved death away out of a window, saw it buzz off into the ether.

But now, entirely out of the blue, the thought of death occurs to Maya as she looks up from her waiting-room chair in the bus depot to confront an expansive derriere drooping into a hammock of frayed denim. So close is Maya, she notices at once the efforts of a gleaming patent leather belt to bolster this dispirited descent. Not so much a belt, she decides, as a bold swagger barely holding up the jeans, with a round gunmetal buckle jostled all the way to the back and gaping open like a hungry mouth. O! A label stitched under the belt reads *LEV* with a smudge over the following letter, *I*. And then the *S*, resurrected from indeterminacy into a squiggle and a flourish, clinching the embroidered calisthenics in a foppish design.

There is something sad about this labored presentation that makes Maya think of endings. So much effort over an inevitable collapse.

I. This is *I*, thinks Maya quickly. *Me. I'm* here. This is today. And I'm here.

The man with the foreboding bottom straightens up and turns around abruptly, his attempts at resurrecting the soda machine in vain. His straggly ponytail tosses from side to side, slapping against his face. *Whap whap!* The sound is oddly pleasant, like water lapping against concrete. He sits down heavily on a bench next to Maya and groans loudly. Or burps. Maya isn't sure, but it is certainly the sort of noise that Maya's mother would have dismissed out of hand as uncouth. Other people's mothers said "gross" or "disgusting." Maya's mother Nina is not Other People.

"Bad language is a creeping canker in the mind," Nina warned Maya. "It will eat away your brain." Maya liked the word "canker." So close to "cancer" and yet so distant, a whiff of Shakespeare closeted in the mouths of people.

Quite possibly this man will talk to her. Ask for money, maybe. Or want to know her name. Or the time. Anything is possible. Maya has come to see this recently when her father left for California without a return ticket, even though it was Maya's eleventh birthday in a few short weeks.

"Got the time?" says the man.

Maya is thinking of birthday cake, pink with white roses. The question hangs over the cake like an affront. The man shifts urgently toward her on his too-narrow bench as if negotiating a treaty with a challenging opponent.

Maya weighs her options. She could move away or glance at her watch (which she already did a minute ago) and say "Six forty-five" in a businesslike way because such requests burden a thinking woman who has places to go. White sugar with eleven roses, one more for luck maybe, but never thirteen, because thirteen is unlucky. Her father left on the thirteenth of March on a zooming airplane.

Years ago, Maya's parents left India for the United States on the thirteenth day of a lunar fortnight. An auspicious number that promises good fortune and eternal happiness, Nina often repeated with more than a tinge of irony. But this is another country, and Maya knows numbers can be confusing in different applications. Her math test grades frequently make that clear.

The thirteenth of March is definitely not lucky.

"Almost the Ides," her mother had said bitterly to Maya, who thought "Theides" was a Greek word she must look up in the dictionary. She would not ask her mother to explain. Nina's sudden bursts of fury kept questions at bay as if they were hungry wolves to be beaten back. Maya had to be quiet and reserved, which was much the way Greek goddesses (the nicer ones) behaved in stories. They survived all odds. Maya was a Greek goddess when not in school or doing homework. Theides, Goddess of Daddies.

"Six forty-five," says Maya firmly to the man now looking straight at her.

The bus depot is almost empty, the waiting room musty with old cardboard boxes, faded vinyl chairs, and the dingy smell of departure. Maya can almost taste the sourness of the place. She coughs to clear her throat, wondering whether Theides ever coughed. Or sneezed. Or blew her nose. Greek goddesses might deal death or pestilence, but they rarely made unseemly noises. Maya will have to ask her mother after Nina recovers from her fits of anger, though this possibility seems far away, at least for now.

The man is still staring at her, taking inventory. Maya looks back at him, aware of what he sees. A skinny kid with a tic at the side of her mouth, throbbing up and down like a pulse in the wrong place. Brown saucer eyes lined in pencil. A small twitchy nose. Frilly pink shirt and black leggings. Long black hair.

"I'm Dan," he says. He doesn't expect an answer. The information is presented as an incontrovertible fact. "My baby girl," he adds. "Ethelbertha. You're kinda like her."

Maya is startled by this unsolicited observation.

"Ethelbertha," repeats Maya. The name seems to squat bossily on her, though she can't quite tell why.

"Ee-yup," says the man. "Ethel as in my mother's name, and Bertha as in my ex's mom. Ethelbertha. All grown up now."

"Oh," says Maya. She has no idea where this conversation is going. "Are you on your way to see her?"

"Nah," says the man. "My ex is gone with Ethelbertha. Haven't seen them in some time. Long time. And my son, David. All gone, the whole damn shebang."

"I see," says Maya politely.

"My baby." The man seems to be lapsing into an elusive memory.

He spreads his hands up and away from him, parting the air gently. His fingers ripple downward in bumpy cascades. "Long black hair she had. Like yours. Reminded me, you know."

He shifts toward Maya, suddenly alert. "But her mom, a bitch."

Maya looks away. Uncouth, her mother would have said. A middle-aged man on a Greyhound bench—a man full of noises—in blue jeans with raggedy holes. His ponytail hangs limply over his shoulder like a comatose skunk. He needs a haircut. And a bath. Maya corrects herself. A bath? Is that too mean to say? Some people are homeless, so they don't have bathrooms. They have shelters with faucets and instructions on the wall in black letters: USE WATER SPARINGLY. DO NOT WASTE SOAP. Maya has seen these directions herself in the shelter downtown when she volunteered at Thanksgiving. The people were huddled around the dinner table in overcoats thick as comforters, and yet they seemed cold, shivering as if the winter snows had followed them indoors and melted into their bones. They were not thankful for their dinner. They scoffed at the stringy turkey and dismissed the lumpy mashed potatoes. All the while they held out their plates for more, as if punishment were reprieve. Maya couldn't blame them at all. She was glad to come home to endless hot water baths and clouds of foaming soap.

Mom, she thinks, Mom.

The words burst in her head like faint pellet-gun explosions.

Mommom poppop.

Maya closes her eyes and shifts slightly away from the man, a sign he understands immediately. He has stopped his busy shifting, his face now vacant as a pause.

Not so late at night, not even seven o' clock, and the only other travelers biding their time are two old ladies at the other end of the waiting room, their heads bent into magazines like horses drinking long draughts of water from a paper trough. The ticket booth woman, tight yellow curls over a wizened face, is hidden behind the bars, a caged monkey chattering brightly to herself. Or so it seems to Maya. Lost in la-la or cell phone land.

"No, no, Jimmy," she cries excitedly. "*You* go first!"

Her voice streams out of the ticket booth in a thin continuous breath—*ugofust!*—a word that sounds like an exotic disease to Maya. *Theides was felled by ugofust, a creeping canker in the mind that led to sudden outbursts of fury and stilled all questions.* On the other hand, the smart goddesses survived plagues and being carried off in all directions. Maya ticks them off mentally.

Artemis.

Nemesis.

Athena.

Aphrodite.

Persephone.

Theides, known for her stunning beauty and stoic majesty, overcame the curse of ugofust.

A giggle escapes Maya, but she stops abruptly and concentrates on her existence in this very moment, just as the yoga-and-mindfulness class instructor at the Y suggested that post-cancer Nina practice daily as a calming device. *Center yourself and be still. Feel the peace.*

But Maya's center is growling, softly. But emphatically.

Maya is hungry, has been for hours.

To run away from home requires forethought, not an impulse. Sandwiches and money. A plan. More consideration than telling your mother yesterday that you'd be at a sleepover at Jenny's, best friend and almost-close-as-a-sister. And then skipping the school bus to hitch a ride instead to the depot with an old farmer in a rusty Buick. Hitching the ride reminded Maya of a statuette Nina once showed her in *National Geographic* of Athena, her mouth opened wide and marble arm held high, as if in perpetual victory or calling a taxi. A super-goddess with a practical side, something to be desired.

"You goin' somewhere?" asks the blue-jean man, lightly, tracing an invisible spider that seems to be running up and down his left arm. "Or just waitin' for someone?"

Maya doesn't answer. She is distracted by the old ladies, who speak suddenly, as if on cue.

"Chocolate sauce," announces the older and more rotund of the ladies, a lace bonnet perched jauntily on her head. Her blue tulle skirt flows away from her like a scratchy ocean.

"That's what I always say," agrees the other, lost in a voluminous beige dress.

Maya wonders if they are Mennonites.

"*Chocolate sauce* brings it alive," says bonnet-lady emphatically, dismissing dissent even if there isn't any. She rummages in her skirts and brings out a black cellphone as if to call someone, then thinks better of it and drowns the phone again in a rustling swath of tulle.

Beige-dress peers into bonnet-lady's magazine. "And fresh cream with strawberries," she offers self-effacingly. "With a smidge of tarragon."

Bonnet-lady nods approvingly.

Maya realizes they are discussing recipes. She imagines strawberry buoys bobbing amid cream-crested chocolate waves. Her empty stomach growls in sympathetic accompaniment.

A cracked television on the far wall is turned on by the ticket booth woman, who has now arranged her chair in a geometrically challenging way to best view the screen. A newsflash materializes in vivid color, and a worried anchorman tut-tuts about world affairs while smoke rises on the far horizon over a landscape of rubble. Mosul is under attack and has been for the past three days. Two American soldiers have been killed. Sacrificed for freedom, observes the anchor somberly, as light glints off a fusillade of distant gunfire.

"Them furriners," says the ticket booth woman, annoyed. "All them furriners killing people everywhere!" Up goes her arm over her head, waving vigorously to indicate everywhere. "*Who* does that?"

No one answers, so she changes the channel to *Wheel of Fortune*, where a smiling contestant has just won $5,000 and a trip to Aruba.

"Yew Ess Eei," says the man, suddenly galvanized. "Keep 'em out is what I say! Yew Ess Eei! Out I Say!"

Maya squirms away resolutely.

"Difficult times," sighs the lady in beige. "All sacrifice is love. Hebrews 9:22." She pulls nervously at her fingers one by one.

Maya is intrigued. Does she mean Mosul? Not Aruba surely. Unless you poured the fires of one into the blue waters of the other. Peace then, unity across the world.

"I'm goin' to Seattle." The man on the bench is talking, but to whom?

Maya glances around.

To her.

"Where *you* goin'?" The man is insistent as an itch.

Maya's father is in California. The Big C got his emotional knickers in a twist, according to Nina. He was suffocating, he said. Had to get away. Couldn't breathe with all the tension. Secondhand smoke chemo.

A day after his departure, either to temper things or make them worse, Maya's father sent an email explaining his plans to head a startup company in San Jose and, most important, to begin anew. Those were his very words. "Begin anew" sounds more promising than "divorce," at least to Maya's father, who will soon have no wife but possibly girlfriends, possibly golden California girlfriends. Clichéd girlfriends, like his clichéd job. Her mother will have the house in South Bend, her teaching job at the community college, and some bills to pay. She will be bitter but stoic, because anything else is uncouth. Maya can see all this ahead as plain as day, but not if she has a say in it—which she will shortly when she gets to California.

Not to be felled by an email, Nina made an announcement. "Let me lay it all out," she said, sounding like a fecund chicken. This betrayal was for her a kind of death, she said, her voice steady but her eyes glazed over in pain. "He just thinks we can all do as we damn well please," she added. "Starting up? I'd say shutting the hell down. Shutting us all bloody down."

Maya now knows:

1) Sometimes mothers can be Other People. Even *uncouth* when the situation requires.
2) Other Mothers in South Bend, all devoutly Catholic and trailing drifts of hair spray and lavender soap, are more circumspect about absent fathers and tell their children that Daddy is "on vacation" or "just de-stressing." Sometimes they say it while smiling and baking cookies. "HailMaryMotherofGod," they murmur soothingly, holding sugar-icing wands against their breasts, when South Bend daddies get all loud and cranky. But to Maya they said, "You lucky girl! Lucky ducky!"

"You luckyducky girl!" they caroled to Maya in maternal chorus to cheer her up after Nina made the email public a little viciously, accidentally on purpose, by confiding in a loose-lipped neighbor. "You *super* lucky girl to be in America! Where you can be all that you can be! Follow your dream! Have a cookie!"

Maya wants to believe them. These Other Mothers believe in America and Jesus. In America all things are saved if you just believe. You are safe, away from guns and bombs and religious crazies. They read the newspapers. They are kind to Black people. They contribute to the Red Cross. They shut their eyes. They believe.

Maya's mother pays them no attention. Instead she chases down this new threat of death with a few choice curses. Having swatted away the Big C, all other forms of death are metaphorical for Nina. Contestable, but hovering. A buzzing, stinging thing. Mosquitophorical.

Nina is still young, a woman barely past her thirties. She loves her daughter deeply, but with a kind of impatience reserved for uncooperative pets. Back in India, when Nina was a girl herself, she had a cat called Rufus, a feisty tabby. *Decades* ago, says Nina dismissively, though she keeps a photograph of Rufus on her dresser and treats her past as a recoverable Utopia. Maya considers such obsessions morbid. At the very least, unduly sentimental. The cat looks out from the photograph like a feudal lord, distant and a bit testy with the serfs. The photograph is right next to one taken of baby Maya, cherubic in a stiff lace dress.

Maya had a gerbil once, but gave it away before disaster could strike, as apparently it can at any time. Though possibly never in California where the skies are blue and the water infused with vitamins, which is why Maya is headed there. Soon she will smell of lavender and cookies and set up house for her father.

"California," she says finally, less a response to the man than an affirmation of intent.

"You don't say," says the man. He seems impressed. "California's a long ways away for a little girl."

Maya is momentarily disconcerted, not having considered her remark grounds for a conversation. She has no ticket for anywhere, nor (the thought sinks in now, dismays her) the money for one, or even a sandwich. She thinks of the sleepover at Jenny's, and wonders if her mother has called Jenny's parents to check on Maya's whereabouts after her clarinet lesson. Perhaps her watch can be bartered for money. A gold-trimmed watch, a present from her father. She doesn't really need to know the time, anyway. Who will buy her watch? Maya looks around.

Someone new has entered the bus depot. A Black man with a straw hat over a scarred face, two jagged lines reaching up his cheek like branches. His large canvas pants are pulled up to his waist with braids of metal, and around his neck hangs a thick silver chain.

The old ladies stiffen immediately and talk a bit louder.

"James thinks it's always cold in Buffalo, but I think the summers are lovely there." Bonnet-lady is definite about this.

"Never been to Buffalo," says beige-dress. "Though Niagara Falls, that's lovely for sure."

"We were at Niagara Falls," says bonnet-lady, displeased. "For our honeymoon. Not bad. Though for me, Buffalo is still so much nicer. The summers and all."

Maybe these old ladies have just met, are not old friends, possibly not Mennonites, just wayfarers wrapped up warmly for a long bus journey, just biding time exchanging old memories like faded photographs.

The blue-jean man hums softly, tracing the path of his invisible spider up his shirt and into the pulse in his throat. Maya can barely hear him but knows that what he is murmuring isn't good. He begins singing, a rhymeless song with classical notes, something fancy, Mozart or Beethoven. Maya can't tell for sure. But she knows the song has the Word in it, the word that describes other people not like you. The word for Black people. She's heard it before. Once it was shouted out at her by someone in a speeding car as she got off the school bus. Then the car careened back, and a crewcut teenager stuck his head out of the window.

"Dot head!" he shouted, with a connoisseur's need for accuracy.

Her mother waved the incident away. Those are just clueless people, she said, as if they were objects of pity, as if they lived under the earth in another dimension. *Way* beyond uncouth. Maya is hearing the word again now. But this world is real, this dimension.

The man with the silver chain has either not heard the word or merely chosen to ignore it. His attention is drawn to a medley of small noises emanating from the cavernous door behind him, a darkened shell from which things seem to emerge like apparitions. A child has entered the bus depot, a girl, possibly five years old, tap-dancing her way toward the new arrival. An elf in a belted gingham sundress, bobby socks, and spotless white Keds. She has a red ribbon in her curly brown hair and a fetching frown on her face. Her eyes are alert with anticipation.

"I wants candy," says the child as if there are no two ways about it. She pulls at her ribbon.

Bonnet-lady is transfixed by the dancing child. "A child shall lead us," she murmurs.

"A dear little lamb," agrees beige-dress. "The blood of innocents saves us. It washes our robes and makes them white."

"Amen," they say together, glancing nervously at the man next to Maya who is now singing louder.

He may be insane. This is a new and unsettling thought for Maya, and the shadows in the depot are beginning to look strange, stretching out across the room in long fingers. The room's three bulbs pool light randomly, as if on whim. The cavern door yawns open, a hungry maw. The woman in the ticket booth has disappeared, and a telephone rings out, a clear bell. Nobody answers the phone, but at least it drowns out the man's singing.

"Ain't no candy here." Astonishingly, the new arrival seems to be this girl's father.

Candy would be good. Maya pulls in her aching stomach to stop it from rumbling. A Snickers bar. A roll of gumdrops. One gumdrop. Anything.

The girl's father drops three coins into the soda machine.

"There's soda." He shakes the broken machine halfheartedly. "Or none."

The child ignores him and sits down across from Maya in a metal chair.

"You gots candy?"

Maya shakes her head.

"My mom gots candy," says the child accusingly. "She *always* gives me candy."

This is a new experience for Maya, being the grown-up in a conversation. Usually it's others who shape the give-and-take with her. She's free to answer any which way, leaving her parents' fellow immigrant

Indian friends to consider their next response so they look like they're interested, or at least polite. When you are almost eleven, grown-ups chat in a stream of questions, as if gathering data:

"So how is school these days?"

"Do you like math?"

"Do you want to be a doctor or an engineer?"

Maya and the child eye each other. The man next to her on the bench is digging under his fingernails with a wooden toothpick. His nails are darkly fungal, and he appears committed to their cleaning. The woman at the booth has gone away, it seems. The child's father (or so he must be) is pulling out luggage from under a bench, two tired suitcases as battered as his face. Only in leather the damage is appealing, suitcases with stories of places to tell. The two old ladies are distracted, watching everyone, but especially Maya and the child. They are whispering to each other.

Wssswsss. The *wsss*-ing sounds like a secret to be shared. A shushing, a hissing. What is the secret? Maya sees it now. Her father is right here in the room!

Maya sees him clearly, with his briefcase held aloft and advancing toward her. He's just the way she last saw him, in exactly the same brown tweed business suit, wafting the same evening smell of aftershave smudged with sweat. Just before he made his California announcement and mentioned signing papers to her mother. Before he chucked Maya under the chin said she was always his girl. Simple, like that. And then gone.

But here he is! Maya rises up in joy. *I'm here! I'm here!* she thinks. *You found me!*

She stumbles over the man's foot in her haste, not seeing the room at all. Her haste has cast a spell, and now her father has disappeared. *It's my fault*, thinks Maya. *It's my fault again.*

"Hey now," says the blue-jean man, not unpleasantly and in an almost familiar way, as if addressing an old pal on a park bench. "The bus ain't here yet. Someplace else to go?"

The question is a revelation to Maya. A place to go!

Maybe her father is hiding behind the ticket booth, on the other side where there is just a narrow strip of space and a cardboard carton that almost fills it. That's where he'd go to keep out of sight. Maybe he's hiding there now. When she was little, he'd hide in places he knew she'd look so Maya could always find him. Under the stairs, under the beds, behind the drapes, in a box. She'd run into the backyard, look up, scouring the sky. He could be there, hanging loose on the moon, perched on a star. Or underground, tunneling to China with a silver spoon. He was sudden and anywhere, he was, like a breath or a jump, like a laugh or a sneeze. He made life easy and full of surprises, just as it should be. "Shut your eyes," he'd say, "and count to ten!" And then she'd find him, laughing, his head tossed back, jubilant as Shiva blazing out of the sky and ready to swallow the ocean. He'd pick her up and swing her around in a dizzying whirl. All chaos then and piggybacks. Amen and sugar icing. As it was then, it will be now and forever. Maya will make it so. She steps past the child and heads toward the booth.

Wssswsss, signal the ladies, bending and drifting like willows, hurry on now, you'll find him. The blue-jean man is watching her, curious.

"You take care now," he calls out genially, like a game show host.

Maya squeezes behind the booth, into the narrow space against the wall. Her father is not here.

She is, though, and can wait. The cardboard carton is empty, inviting her to fill it.

No one can see her. Everybody's on the other side of the booth. It's just her now, waiting. She gets into the box and it fits her—like a mitten, she thinks—all curled up, a fist. She pulls off her gold-trimmed watch and it clatters into the box; she does not need the time. She will burrow deep into her center. She will feel the peace.

Soon a scrape of wheels. A commotion again, louder now, with the thudding of bags and chatter. The depot has come to life. Small rivulets of color rise up swiftly from the floor and burst into rainbow hues that spurt through the air, leaving in their wake a trail of feathers and light. Puffs of melody rise and fall, swirling together and blending in soft crescendos. Everything is immediate and still so far away. Maya struggles to see through this haze. Any moment now the police will arrive—she has no doubt of this—and her mother with Jenny-who-can-never-keep-a-secret, who will tell on her, who is her best friend and almost-sister and a wuss. As if on cue, a police car siren cleaves the air merrily to the tune of "Oh Happy Day!" and a rush of voices engulfs Maya in spangled confetti. Then the light clears and the music falls.

"You here, kid?" Flashlights flood the box. "She's here! Get her out!" A portly, bustling policeman with a red face and cape looks like Santa with a gun. And now her mother arrives in a rush, sari pallav flying, arms outstretched and zooming like an angel through the air. "I believe!" Maya calls out to her mother. "I *believe!*"

The highway journey is full of laughter. The police car is stacked to the roof with mounds of candy bars and rolls of gumdrops. The policeman is a jolly fellow, singing loudly and promising hot chocolate and a teddy bear. Nina holds her daughter close. They are home.

A Greyhound bus is leaving. The room is very quiet. The box is sharper than she ever imagined cardboard could be, corrugated like a man's scarred face. The candy-obsessed child, her father, Maya wonders where they are.

When she opens her eyes, maybe a minute later, maybe hours, she sees the man in the dirty blue jeans looking down at her. She looks back up at him from within the box, a baby bird.

There is no sound in the bus depot, not even the whispers of the old ladies. Not even a tick-tock clock. There is nothing but the man looking down at her, as if he wants to help.

"You okay, kid?" he says.

His jeans show portholes at the knees. He turns to pick up something from the floor. A soda can. So close again, she sees the *I'S* after the *LEV* under his belt quite clearly now, even in the dimmed light of the room.

He has the soda can in his hand. He jerks it awkwardly toward her.

"Want some?" His fingernails are polished clean as razor blades.

There is no sound in the depot, just the lulling sense of Sunday afternoons when her mother ran Maya a bath, the soapsuds light and airy, magic bubbles to carry her away—to California or India or wherever you damn well pleased. Maya would sink into the water and pretend she was deep in the sea where there were no fishes, just the rush of water swishing past her ears. She'd lie there without moving while her parents laughed and talked behind the door, their voices filtering through the steam on wisps of foam. If she lifted her arms, Maya could pull herself up like a mermaid or a goddess, Theides rising up out of the water and into the air, up, and up, and up into the light.

"Need help?"

The man is even closer, bending urgently over the box. His ponytail hangs down, a lifeline for her to clamber up. He is scratching at an army of spiders on his left arm. How they hurry, up and down! She can smell his musty breath. His metal belt buckle gapes open like a welcome, a moon to hang loose on, a mouth ready to swallow the ocean.

The water flows away from Maya in great big sheets, and she is all alone. She is on a breaker by the beach, looking out into a vast and careless sky. Not a cloud, not a breeze, just a dipping silence like at the bottom of the sea. If she calls, will her father see her, bring her candy, chocolate sauce, a birthday present? She doesn't doubt this for one moment. Yes, of course he hears her. If she shuts her eyes, he will.

Temporary Shelters

Woodsmoke and Lime

Winter was only a trace away. We knew when the seasons turned because the limes Mother had pickled took on their sourest tang. And we lived through days of cold and lime freshness. It was a combination I never found again, though I sniffed the air with anticipation through the years.

That was the time my uncle Chinoy came to stay with us. He was the thrall of summer, spilling warmth like an overcrowded beach. We children dispensed with order, buzzed like kites over our parents, who struggled to reel us in with dire exhortations. To no avail. The days spooled out endlessly, golden through that summery winter. When Chinoy left at the end of the season with Mother's earrings and the family jewel box, I was sorry. We were told by Father to consider the matter from a moral point of view and see what a rascal the fellow was. We saw. If a man could invert the seasons and lift Mother's diamonds with such aplomb, he had to be a genius. We informed neighborhood children that Uncle stole in order to give to the poor. Just like Robin Hood, we said.

Father remained unimpressed by our attempts at distributing edifying public information and paddled us soundly for lying. In the interests of survival, such retribution immediately adjusted my moral perspective.

Sitting on the front porch almost forty years later, I said to my husband that Father's wrath pushed me over the threshold. A kind of ritual passage, I remarked. A crossing. My husband, for whom Uncle was merely a spirit behind yellowing photographs of children trapped on a roof, a presence denoted entirely by absence, only grunted in reply.

But all this was much later, after time had winnowed our instincts. Then all we had was our anticipation as we huddled in our lichee tree house one October afternoon, speculating with thrilling abandon on Uncle's physiognomy. The possibilities were endless. A giant gnome with superhuman abs. A flying walrus in purple suspenders and a grass skirt. Less exciting, just a starving professor in his dusty garret scratching out yet another PhD on the therapeutic effects of scented candlewax. Disdaining buttered toast and similar vulgar sustenance, hungry and discouraged by his lumpy turns of academic phrase, he turned mean at the stroke of every midnight and devoured children—a revelation that required vigorous fanning and a lollipop to revive my little sister Anu. Captive to our imagination, anticipation guttered into apprehension. This turnabout endeared us immediately to Father.

Being our mother's second cousin once removed distanced Chinoy further from our affections. Another jobless hanger-on, we thought.

"What does he do, Sushila?" demanded Father at breakfast one morning.

"He's a poet," said Mother vaguely. "Or perhaps a palmist. Or a photographer. Or is he working on a novel?"

I was delighted, anticipating my own imagined talents would find a sympathetic ear.

Father snorted and rustled his paper, behind which he always took refuge at moments of intense crisis, usually before the arrival of Mother's relations.

"Once removed!" he muttered darkly, as if the connection were undeniably diabolic. When Mother informed him of the impending domestic invasion timed for five o'clock by the evening train from Delhi, Father rustled the paper vigorously. It was the sound of defeat. Mother won all her battles. Father was all rustle and no boom. He faded out before her quiet resoluteness.

While Mother ordered a WelcomeChinoy chocolate cake from the the HolyWood Bakery, I attempted a verse to herald his arrival:

Chinoy is a mystery man,
A palmist, poet, novelist;
An uncle, friend, a puzzlement
A man who cannot pay the rent.

The effort was unsatisfactory, so I turned it into a paper plane and aimed it at Chotu Sharma, our unfavorite sidekick neighbor sitting on the wooden fence between our houses. He ran home to tell his mother.

And so Chinoy arrived light on cat feet later that day, swinging a duffel bag and a grungy old box camera (which he swore would work), his fingers sparkling with three diamond rings. To celebrate, Mother cut us each a large piece of bakery cake, which was enough to sweeten both our palate and our perceptions. Disappointingly neither gnome nor hungry professor, Chinoy looked benign enough for Anu to observe he was definitely vegetarian.

Father immediately discounted this possibility. "Jobless people eat anything," he explained to Anu. "Even the shirt off your back."

Momentarily mystified though she was by the dietary habits of the jobless, Anu focused her attention on Uncle, who was distributing brown packages from the bag. The first held a pair of long johns embroidered generously with red hearts, a present for Father. ("No thanks," said Father shortly, "I prefer boxers myself.") The second, a silk scarf for Mother. The third, a bottle that passed without explanation, though we waited for enlightenment. Father looked at us severely and said, "Ah! Tonic water!" in a tone of loud appreciation. The last package was the best. It held crunchy mints that we demolished in minutes while Uncle made paper boats from the wrapping paper and told us stories of the magical forests of Sherwood. In his version, the Merrie Men lounged on beds of asphodel and drank elixir, while grateful peasants feted them with gifts of frankincense and myrrh.

Years later, after Chinoy had died in an accident, I thought first of the forests. He had led a charmed life in his wilderness of dreams. Magic doesn't last forever, as we grew to learn through stolid office hours and endless bickering with husbands. But that winter Chinoy was young and handsome, with a sudden devastating dimple that flashed warmth at us like an intermittent beam from a lighthouse. It disarmed everybody except Father, who distrusted dimples and their illogical efficacy of persuasion.

Dimples and vodka are a combustible combination. As if to prove the point, Chinoy depleted the contents of the bottle, punctuating the intervals between swigs with reflective sighs. We thought the performance fetching. Father made a pot of coffee, which he then emptied with a religious intensity. That Him, This Me, he indicated by brandishing a brimming coffee cup like a ceramic staff, Moses parting the empty air.

Though we didn't know it yet, the swigging was merely the prelude to a main event. Chinoy got riotously drunk, much to our sympathy and Father's rage. He provided us with a stirring display of theatrics, our introduction to Shakespeare. Convinced he was Mark Anthony, Chinoy bounded up onto the roof, where he spoke heartrendingly on the merits of friendship and gratitude to a small but appreciative audience of action-starved neighbors.

"Hurrah! Zindabad!" shouted Chotu, all manly ten-year-old vigor, while his mother pursed her lips and narrowed her eyes, afraid we might thread his hair with ribbons or tie him to a lichee tree yet again.

The diamonds on Chinoy's fingers blazed with moral authority. Father took the occasion as a personal attack for having refused the underwear, especially when Chinoy swathed his head in the long johns and executed a spirited bhangra, accompanying his efforts with banshee howls and whistles. When restored to propriety by the Fire Department and several ice packs, he spent a penitent weekend nursing a hangover and mulling over Father's vociferous charge of him being a useless no-good godforsaken hanger-on.

Father never quite recovered from the trauma of a cavorting Mark Anthony, and his admonitions were henceforth concluded with the cryptic adult pronouncement "Besides, the fellow's always drunk."

If God had forsaken Chinoy, he was unaware of any such perfidy, and to prove his innocence and annoy Father, Chinoy brought to our attention a small roadside temple ringing gently with bells, the air inside blurred with camphor. We never went there to pray, because my parents believed in worship without recourse to external aids. Chinoy professed amazement.

"Prayer," he explained to Father, "rises from the soul but must soar freely into the elements to merge with the Infinite, as the Vedas teach us. I am a poet. I know these things."

Father said something incoherent about the monthly income of poets.

"Children must pray in the fields and meadows," continued Chinoy, undeterred, "to truly experience God's universe. *Om tat sat.* They grow with outdoor worship," he added mysteriously, "like plants in sunlight."

We were affected differently by the organic metaphor. I saw myself in the mind's eye as a daffodil chanting the Lord's Prayer, while Father humbly begged forgiveness for burying his children in the muddy depths of domestic privacy. But Chinoy remained impervious to innuendo, even when Father inquired, "And what do they grow on? Vodka?" Instead, and with considerable panache, he organized a procession to the temple. We soon discovered why. There were coconuts, agarbathi, oil, and lamps to be carried to and fro. My mother's family prefers management to labor.

A strange sight met us through the open window. Here was Chinoy, gracefully draped over an armchair, hooking a teacup with the pinkie of his injured hand while airily waving the other arm about as if swatting away attacking armies. His diamond-studded fingers sparkled, tossing sunlight on the walls. Chinoy was entertaining female company. She was large and friendly, calm and unpretentious as a motherly hippo.

The next thought that struck us was that she was Sylvie D'Souza, the girl with the Reputation. Anyone seen with the Reputation, if male and over fifteen, was eternally damned. We blanched in righteous moral horror. But Anu, for whom anything maternal exerted magnetic attraction, ran inside and jumped on Sylvie's lap.

A terrified silence followed. Then we all said hello in a hurry, noticing that the fracture had miraculously healed. The bandages on the floor were actually Chinoy's long johns. The red hearts leered at us.

"How did it get well so soon?" demanded Anu, sensing a conspiracy.

"God?" Chotu Sharma was awed.

"That is correct," said Chinoy. "All the while you were at the temple, I was on my knees, praying. Praise be to God! A Miracle!" He pressed the palms of his hands together. "Now tootle along."

A squeal from Sylvie indicated unexpected company. The front door opened, and it seemed to me that in an instant my parents, Chinoy, and Sylvie all rushed together into a frenzied, blurry ball, arms and legs flailing, as if they were cartoon characters under captions like BAM! and POW! The reality was less exciting, just a brief, shouting conference. As Father emerged from the encounter, dizzy but defiant, we concluded he'd viewed the Miracle without awe.

Peesanluv! Recognizing the urgent need for this imperative, Anu pointed out the obvious. "Look, Daddy! Poor Uncle's been sick in bed with the nurse, drinking tonic water."

"And his parents in-cul-*kay*-ted faith," I added. This was getting better by the minute. "He was just trying to be more-cul-*kay*-ted."

73

"Inebriated!" Hell had risen and peopled Father's home with devils. "Inebriation, and worse! Is this an example for our children?"

But Father's inquiry buzzed aimlessly like static in the air because Chinoy had, by this time, made an admirably hasty exit through the French windows.

That night while Father paced and raged and Chinoy braced himself for another penitent hung-over weekend, we prayed devoutly for a share in the mysterious grace accorded to the chosen. Over the next few days, we exercised our powers.

"Abracadabra!" we cried in unison, violently brandishing broomsticks over Rufus like an orgy of orchestra conductors. "Abracadabra! Fee fi fo fum! Tiddlywinks! Supercalifragilistic! Turn into a frog! Disappear! Become an ice cube and melt!"

Rufus flipped his tail and yawned.

Chinoy was our entrance to romance and adventure and to the authenticity of dreams. Visiting relatives, obliged to entertain us, took us to Napoli Restaurant for tutti-frutti ice cream or to the Odeon cinema for a chopped-up Disney film. Once, to our delight, we saw *Cinderella* in reverse order, the last reel first. Sometimes we stopped by the English Book Depot on Rajpur Road to pick up an Archie comic book, or a shiny Enid Blyton paperback. Visiting relatives were a capitalist's treasure, a goldmine of Christmas-come-early. But Chinoy shrugged off such plebian pleasures. Instead, he read our palms by moonlight, promising us crazy husbands, seafaring journeys, and troves of hidden gold. He took us camping on the Siwalik Hills where we spent two hours lighting an obstinate heap of wood. The wood finally caught fire, but the smoke was so bitter we had to run downhill in a hurry, choking and gasping. Another time he climbed onto the roof to retrieve a cricket ball. We followed suit and got stuck on the roof. While we bawled, anticipating death, Chinoy took photographs, convinced of the moment's historic significance. Father was obliged to summon the Fire Brigade again, much to the entertainment of bored neighbors who had been anticipating some sort of encore performance.

"Don't make a habit of this, Mr. Menon," said the fire chief to Father. "Take up bridge."

"Disgraceful!" Father muttered to the hydrant, which remained unmoved. "Fellow wants the children killed. Besides, he's always drunk."

The afternoons were long and quiet that winter, full of the gentle whispers of leaves. Tall trees dipped paternally over us, sighing out their sorrows, old men bent with the winds of passing years. Leaves and trees, swirls of breeze, drifts of sunshine dappling shadows across the plain. And Chinoy was a sharp quickness, a stir in the leaves, trailing in his wake the revelry of summer, the warmth.

One such afternoon, Rufus disappeared. We searched diligently but unsuccessfully behind furniture and under culverts, sleuthing our way through the streets up to the town's clock tower. By six in the evening, we were all as tense as violin strings. Chinoy organized search parties ("Hah!" said Father), and it was he who finally found the cat. Rufus had been dead a few hours, strangled by an unknown sadist and left sprawled in ungainly repose in a roadside ditch. I was too young to really know sorrow, but my sister Nina was growing up and, at eleven, a simmering, yearning girl. Nina and Chinoy didn't come in for dinner, which nobody could eat anyway. I was delegated to look for them.

They were in the garden under a sad black sky of clouds, saying nothing, just gazing together at some vague point in the distance. I sat beside them in order to share this silent mystery, but when mosquitoes descended purposefully on my toes, I beat a quick retreat into the house. My last glimpse was of two shadows, a host of bugs, and a dark receding skyline. I still don't know why I wanted to cry, watching them from the lamplit safety of the house, but it had nothing to do with Rufus. Later I knew that in watching them so isolated and together, I had come upon my own first stirrings of loneliness. Through the years it would haunt me, even in the happiest of moments. A sudden gesture, a turn of light, an inflected word. I had just to look around and it would be there, stalking me insidiously like a cat's shadow.

On a late December morning, Chotu's mother strode up to our door, two elderly policemen weighed down by heavy plastic file folders in tow. One policeman was circular horizontally and vertically, the other a stiff rectangle with a gray handlebar mustache. Ponderous geometric shapes, they gazed at us as if their mystery lay beyond the ken of the mathematically inept and could only be deciphered in numbers. Long discharged from the British army, they were now reduced to blowing peremptory whistles at traffic roundabouts in Paltan Bazaar. But their vocabulary remained committed to the Queen. Specifically, Victoria.

"Mr. Chinoy Padmanabhan, Esquire," announced the round one finally, dispelling the Sphinx-like atmosphere by producing a smudged photograph from one of the folders. "Is he quartered here, or out of station?"

"What!" Mother was horrified. "Is someone dead?"

Circle, after an intensive search in another folder, retrieved a warrant for arrest. Chinoy was accused of breaking into a jewelry store in Delhi several months ago. Three diamond rings were missing.

Auntie Sharma clutched dramatically at her throat. Bollywood films were her passion.

Chinoy, she said, had run past her window, just moments before she'd noticed a gold necklace missing from her trinket box. Running like a madman in full view of all neighbors and the gardener, *itna bewakoof!* And then her kitchen furnace had broken down, and the garage roof had sprung a leak! That would be his Evil Eye! *Badtameez!!*

Details grew increasingly muddled and thrilling.

As if in a dream, I watched Chinoy walk downstairs, head held high, an early Christian martyr going to ignorant lions. The dream thickened with shifting images as voices were raised and fists pounded, clearing suddenly when Father shouted, "Get out, you rogue! You've

brought enough shame on the family—and to think we've been shelter-
ing a criminal!"

In the ensuing pause, we quaked in terror—except Anu, for
whom the moment was a Miracle in the making.

"Do something, Chinoy!" she squealed, jumping from foot to
foot. "Just like Merlin! Turn Fatty into a frog! Make Mustaches
disappear!"

Chinoy turned to Anu, but Father held her away.

"Leave my children alone," he said, and this time no one dared
contradict him.

Chinoy appealed to Mother, but she remained silent. For no clear
reason, I had a sudden vision of Father splitting Uncle's skull open like
a coconut, with Mother behind him, applauding. Chinoy's once bejew-
eled fingers were bare, I noticed, and slightly veined and gnarled.

After a pause, Chinoy stirred into life, coming awake after a deep
sleep.

"I'm going," he said, his voice a far-off peal of jangled temple
bells, and the words hung loosely in the air, flapping, lame, an aberration. "I stole nothing—but now I wish I had."

That night I wrote a goodbye poem for Chinoy:

> *Uncle is a puzzlement!*
> *A man who could not pay the rent,*
> *Who took three diamond rings for free*
> *(And a necklace, possibly).*

This effort wasn't any good either, so I tossed it over the fence into
Auntie Sharma's yard.

She thought I was apologizing on behalf of the family and telephoned Mother to say so as proof of Chinoy's malfeasance.

"A twenty-four-carat necklace," Auntie Sharma said accusingly.
"Given to me by my mother-in-law! A family heirloom to be handed
down through generations."

She added, "I was keeping it for Chotu's wife," which sent us into uncontrollable giggling fits.

"I am so sorry about my children," Mother told her, furiously waving us away from the telephone.

"We all are," agreed Auntie Sharma, without hesitation.

Uncle left the next day after a tame discharge for lack of strong evidence. He left in the night with our jewel box and Sylvie.

"Indian legal system," announced Mustaches, washing his hands of things. He wrote down on a paper that our jewel box was missing and filed it in a third plastic folder. Regarding Sylvie, he noted "Immoral Behavior by Female Party" in the margins of his report. "You may wish to file a case," he said. He knew we wouldn't.

"The thief and immoral rascal," roared Father to Mother. "This is what comes of helping your relatives!"

A swirl of memories assaulted me that day but wouldn't fall into place. I thought of trips to the temple, dimples, camping, Rufus, long shady afternoons and mosquitoes. I saw myself in a tree house anticipating a skirted monster. I saw my father's newspaper scrunched and bundled in his fists, a frail shield against his own inadequacies. I saw the priest clutching his pennies as we left the temple, his thin flanks swathed in the tattered yellow rags, banners of a remnant faith. His or ours, I couldn't tell, even now, looking back over the years. In the distance I heard the neighbors applaud, a smooth dry scattering of praise like pebbles on a tin roof where I seemed permanently trapped.

There were things I might never understand, not if I grew to be a hundred. Across the shadowed plain people crossed each other like drifts of light, holding together in moments. And in that brief, sweet tension, time stood still, defeated by the gossamer power of dreams, the brave fragility of faith. But every beginning includes the end, every summer masks a hidden winter. And with each receding childhood, the spires of Camelot dissolve like elephant clouds in the sky, leaving in the wake of miracles and wonder an indefinable emptiness, a threshold. And with the paddling, I finally crossed over, the light behind me, eager to meet my new and terrible self.

Chinoy's stay with us was the quick rustle of leaves on a warm afternoon. Then the weather changed, and we forgot him. We learned, months later, he had gone to America, where amid the snows of Minnesota he opened an Indian restaurant and fed steaming Chicken Mughlai to baffled Swedes. But we forgot him. What remained for years was his old box camera, which was soon abandoned in the corner of the garage. And his embroidered long johns, a handy rag to polish bicycle handles. After this useful career, we children hung them up reverently on a garage peg. There they remained for years, the grimy hearts stoic witness to the forests of asphodel and myrrh.

One September evening decades later, an email arrived. Chinoy had died in a car accident, drag racing in St. Paul, after a drop too much of whisky. Little wonder, I told my husband, the fellow was always drunk. But sometimes even now I think of him briefly. When the smell of bitter woodsmoke comes down the hill. Or with the sharp winter tang of lime.

Coda: Maharajah Abdullah

Most appalling of all was the name he gave his restaurant. For most immigrant entrepreneurs, an exotic hook to the old country was all it took to bring in the natives and flatter their sense of wisdom. Hence the myriad Bombay Curry Houses and Taj Mahal Tandoori Palaces that dotted the national landscape. Personal names missed the spot. The Jawaharlal Nehru Café was mistaken for a coat shop with coffee. That was the truth and not just an anti-Congress joke. But Chinoy was an imaginative man and disdained the obvious. He recognized the formula. Popular title + restaurant + happy patrons = success. And therefore: big house, Toyota, etc. But he rejected it. In his view, part of the immigrant's burden was to educate the masses, elevating them to subtler cultural recognitions so that they might better appreciate their chicken makhani and aloo roti. The restaurant name must be a veil opening to reveal vistas of history, not a guide-post to a menu.

So it was particularly disappointing to the Indian community in St. Paul when Chinoy, after much cogitation, named his restaurant Maharajah Abdullah. This was wrong on so many levels. St. Paul residents could say Maharajah only by separating each syllable. The results were unhappy. "Ma-Ha-Ra-Jah," they said, turning the word into a mediaeval chant or a horse at an easy canter. And Abdullah was oxymoronic. Muslims were Sultans or Shahs. Hindus could be Ambujas or Amaravallis. Certainly not Abdullahs.

"Who has a combined Hindu-Muslim name?" demanded Mrs. Protima Lal, wife of Dr. Shivaji Lal, MBBS, to the Tuesday night prayer session at the mandir. "Only converts!"

Earlier in the evening at the restaurant's grand opening, Chinoy addressed a hungry crowd. "I aim for Hindu-Muslim unity. This is my subtext to opening Maharajah Abdullah."

Chinoy was taking night classes in literary criticism at the University of Minnesota. Words like "subtext," "hegemony," and "subaltern" fell gracefully from his lips but landed like bricks on the heads of fellow immigrants.

"Subtext bubtext," exclaimed Mrs. Lal warmly when apprised of the quote. "As if we are stupid or what? The man is an ulloo."

"Double ulloo," agreed Mrs. Manjula Singh. "Show-offer!"

"All the Americans are laughing at us," said Mr. Gyan Chand, retired lawyer and father of six daughters all at Harvard. "As if we don't know our own culture!"

"That I do not think," said Dr. Thottam, "because Americans, they do not know so many differences. But who is this Maharajah Abdullah? He is not a person."

"That much is definite," said Mr. Gyan Chand.

"Maybe he was like Akbar," said Mrs. Singh, softening. "Perhaps he was someone for unity? Such people are not so popular these days."

The Tuesday evening prayer group turned as one and gazed at Mrs. Singh. She understood her transgression and sneezed politely into her handkerchief.

"Anyway," she said, "The rasgullas at the restaurant are so bad, like big rocks. My son brought some home to play marbles. For that they are very good."

At the renunciation of her apostasy, a swell of appreciation like a lift of song rose and drifted around the room. Orchestrating a finale, Mrs. Lal strummed her santoor for the next bhajan and myriad mouths opened to harmonize.

It was a dream of Chinoy's, from the time he was seven. The house in Bangalore where he grew up was a strange house indeed, built and added to for a hundred years. There were windows that opened into other rooms, a door that led into a wall. Three bedrooms ran one into the other, so Chinoy was forced to mumble an apology twice before reaching his own bedroom at the far end, often frustrating his married cousin and other young couples in their early dip of sleep. In the hall upstairs, the floor offered a sudden patch of glass, a leftover from a skylight before the upstairs was added to the house. The astrologer said it was bad luck for seventy years to break glass in this spot, in these spatial dimensions, and rather than curse her coming generations, his grandmother Amama had sanctified the floor with a coir carpet and a light plastic flowerpot placed thoughtfully over the pane to protect Chinoy and his boisterous friends from unexpected arrivals downstairs. In the pantry was the mango box, in which green mangoes were stored through the summer until they grew yellow and luscious to the touch. At the bottom of the box was a door that led into a dark underground space, eight feet by ten.

"To guard your ancestors," said the maidservant, "in the monsoon season when the winds are too strong for the spirits to fly."

"For hay," said Amama crisply. "To ripen mangoes all year round."

Chinoy chose his own truths. The ancestors slept through the monsoon season and then they traveled the house through the door in the wall into the third bedroom where he slept. There they swirled magic charms above his head until he was forever changed from boy to thing unknown, a page in a book, a paper boat, a deer in a forest. Chinoy's secret life began by default, the legacy of a house without planning. And if his life sometimes rested in contradictions, that was why it made sense to him. Maharajah Abdullah was the perfect name for a restaurant. Its impossibility opened every window into a room.

Some years later in a different country and face to face with Mrs. Lal, he attempted to explain himself.

"In my grandmother's house," he said, "all the rooms were as if made by a mad builder. Those were the happiest days of my life."

Mrs. Lal looked concerned. She furrowed her brow slightly because Chinoy had depleted a bottle of Chianti in minutes. Happiness or the memory of such followed quickly, usually complemented by loud bawling.

"My husband can help you," she said. "He has medicines for all ailments."

The Indian community in St. Paul was growing by the month. By the mid-eighties, doctors and engineers and graduate students were arriving in airplanes, crumpled and harassed at first, but soon spruced and articulate. To speed business, names were condensed and homes expanded. Ashish Chandrasekharan no longer lived at Apartment 12B on Married Student Housing Lane; after four years and a blossoming consultancy, Ash Chandra found sound lodgings on Severn Drive. Mita Mahalanobis tossed off her Indian groom (though green card pending) and married Lawrence "Skip" Hopkins. They had a baby girl in a year and lived happily ever after, including triennial visits to India. Skip loved Hindi films and Rabindranath Tagore, but most of all his family. Chinoy entered a world on the verge of its own remaking, perfect for a man with a past and wit but no prospects.

One evening, five months after his arrival, while sitting in a friend's basement apartment with several fellow LitCrit graduate students and losing a round of bridge, the thought came to Chinoy. A restaurant.

He growled these words aloud. *Urrrestaurant!*

His friend eyed him warily. "You're losing, *yar*," he said. "You owe me six dollars."

"With a restaurant," said Chinoy, "the dough comes rolling in."
"Money," agreed his friend, "is the Chief Masala."

Chinoy had only three hundred dollars. But he had a 24-carat gold necklace, a jewelry box, and three diamond rings.

He also knew a Miss Mehta better than her parents thought he did.

"The Mehtas will help me," he said half to himself. "Manju Mehta is going to Delhi to look for a bridegroom sometime in the summer." His friend's eyes narrowed. The graduate students shuffled their cards. "I will not be getting married soon," explained Chinoy. "Sylvie is waiting for me in India."

"It will be a long wait," said his friend. "Six dollars."

With help from the local bank, the Mehtas, and less identifiable sources, Chinoy rented a small hall on Main Street with the ceiling caving in slightly on the left end and the windows grimy with the sludge of an unrented winter. Once a Chinese restaurant, the hall plus kitchen was now a warehouse for the city municipality. Papers, shoes, machinery, typewriters lay strewn on the floors.

"Like my house," said Chinoy, but who knew he meant that literally.

On either side was a fine line of specialty shops, cheese and wine and bread, a row of boxy faces with freshly washed windows all looking the right way onto the street.

In two weeks Chinoy had hired a cook from New York, a student thrown off his engineering fellowship for reasons never explained. Pandurangan cooked sambhar, idli, and dosa as well as all the required Mughlai dishes that Indian restaurants in the West advertised as pan-Indian food. He was a find, though a temporary one. Pandurangan was hoping for a teaching assistantship at UCLA to be finalized by the next year. It all depended upon a skittish professor unimpressed by Pandurangan's NYU record but still intrigued by his potential.

On Mondays a van from Chicago brought dried lentils, wheat flour, and tubs of fresh yogurt. Chicken and lamb were supplied by the local dealer. Rice poured in from a Vietnamese retailer in Minneapolis.

"How you did this I'll never know," said Chinoy's friend.

"That's fair to say," said Chinoy.

The grand opening was a sight no Indian living in St. Paul on the twenty-third of June, 1983, could fail to remember. Chinoy had hired a shehnai player, a high school student with an Indian mother, whose amateur wailing was mistaken for talent by onlookers availing themselves of Eastern exotica. Manju and her sister were conscripted to wear shimmering bloodred lehengas and provide an energetic performance that proved to be more a Bollywood tribute to Middle Eastern belly dancing.

"How shameless," whispered Mrs. Singh, whose son was to appropriate the rasgulla marbles in an hour or two. "All these young girls these days just wriggling their bottoms in public. You think they would do this in India?"

"We are in a different culture," murmured Mrs. Lal, "So we must adjust."

Mrs. Singh and Mrs. Sobti looked upon her meaningfully while Manju and her sister moaned in ecstasy and sank swirling to the floor to the vibrating din of the shehnai.

"Oh," said Mrs. Lal, and sneezed politely.

At the end of the dance sequence, a crowd of children appeared in costumes of various kinds. One was the Spirit of India, wrapped in the orange, white, and green of an Indian flag.

"I am the Spiricherinjer," he informed the crowd ringing the front door to Maharajah Abdullah. "I am Peace and Seek-You-Ler Unity."

"What he said?" demanded Mr. Gyan Chand, whose lawyerly past had given him a taste for the accurate.

"I think he is looking for something," whispered Mrs. Lal. "It is hard to say."

"I am Sarojini Naidu," said a poised little girl in a blue sari, tossing sheaves of paper around in a version of a rain dance. "I am a poetess, I write good poems, and I am famous."

"Say some poetry," called out a suspicious small boy in the crowd.

The little girl looked downcast.

"I forgot it," she said, and was hustled away by Chinoy.

While small children came and went, Mr. Gyan Chand grew pensive.

"What has this to do with food?" he demanded. "When is the restaurant going to open?"

Mahatma Gandhi was now center stage.

"Such bad taste," observed Mrs. Singh with satisfaction. "As if Gandhiji would open a restaurant. Especially one serving meat!"

A murmur of assent went around the Indian community.

The American well-wishers were more encouraging. "Isn't he sweet?" said Ginny Macdowell from Minneapolis, who had traveled to St. Paul just for the occasion.

Mahatma Gandhi was a pudgy boy of ten wrapped in a white SuperPlush Kmart bath towel.

"I'm wearing a dhoti," he informed the American section of the crowd, "because I am a good and simple man."

The Americans applauded.

"I wanted to wear a shirt," he said, "because it is a bit cold. But my mommy said no."

He was hustled away by Chinoy.

At the very end came Chinoy with a globe in his hands and a long black cape shimmering with sequins.

"Friends, brothers, sisters," he said. "Today is a historic day for the St. Paul community. Today we extend our hearts, and our appetites"—he winked—"to one and all in this wonderful city we all call home. Today we open our hearts, and hence our restaurant door—"

"He is getting on my nerves," whispered Dr. Thottam.

"—to one and all. Come and sample our glorious heritage from India! Here it lies, on your plate. Learn about the glory of a strong and powerful nation, where every subaltern resists the hegemonic rule of the oppressor in ways immediate and symbolic. My hope is to challenge existing stereotypes of the India you see imaged in Books by British Authors and Other Colonialists—"

At this point the two British tourists in the crowd began mumbling audibly. "I think we just need a cuppa," said one. "I'm really not up for dinner."

"—by showing you how a well-cooked Indian meal can bring the powerful and the powerless together in one act of solidarity."

"What the hell he is talking about?" inquired Mr. Gyan Chand, but was drowned out by the waves of applause. Chinoy lifted up his globe and tossed his cape to the right like a tipsy bat.

"Let us take joy in a good meal!" he cried. "I hereby open Maharajah Abdullah!"

"Hear! Hear!" cried the British tourists uncertainly, and everyone else clapped, except Mr. Gyan Chand and Dr. Thottam. The children held hands and sang the national anthem while the local newspaper cameramen took photographs.

(The headline next day in the paper's LifeTimes section read "Young Indian Entrepreneur Uses Food as Metaphor for Protest," which was not quite Chinoy's intention. Nonetheless, it was publicity and brought in local academics committed to eating for worthy causes.)

Later that night Chinoy asked his friend if his speech was really that bad.

"No," said his friend. "Worse."

"Why didn't you stop me?" demanded Chinoy.

"Six bucks," said his friend.

It was a dream of Chinoy's from the time he was seven. He wanted to own the future, to step out and breathe it in. He wanted to intercept and command each day, his fingers tingling with success. He wanted to toss marigolds and incense up into the air and have money come tumbling down. He wanted to read, to know, to change the world with his knowing.

And so when he was at the far edge of youth at thirty-four, with the old crazy house gone, demolished and remade into neat, logical flats with clear windows all facing the street and doors that opened into rooms, when Amama was dead and his childhood transferred to a boarding school in Ooty, Chinoy decided that he would choose his truth not just for now but for always. So he went from college to job to job, recited poetry and strummed a few notes on a guitar in South Delhi cafés, wore his hair long and looked soulful for pretty girls. Ten years later, he went to live with his cousin Sushila who had her own house in the Himalayan foothills, one without a far third bedroom and with two separate doors to get in, to get out. He lived with his cousin whose children loved him dearly but whose husband did not, so he left the husband mumbling by a fire hydrant. He made paper boats for the children and sailed them in the watery grooves left by the rains on the lawn, and he told the children stories about the forests of Sherwood. He bowed his head in temples when he had no faith, and he once beat senseless a man who had strangled a cat, Rufus, though no one was ever to know of this. And in his truth, he took the world as it came to him, diamond rings and all, because he saw that love and safety were no recompense for the spirits in the wind, and because he saw that contradiction was at the heart of truth. In later years he bought a red Ferrari to offset his gray hair, and he roared up and down the highways outside St. Paul, for by now he was a man with many menus to his name and a love of death and of forgetting. One September evening, not long before he died drag racing down the city streets, he was asked if his life was too risky for an old man. To which he answered no, there was once a plastic potted plant over glass in another country and in another time, and he was to have good luck for a lifetime or at least seventy years. And just before he got into his car and revved the engine to rowdy thunder, he brushed away a swarm of mosquitoes from his windshield, remembering a mourning child under a mosquito-laden sky. But then he shook off the memory like fog, like smoke, and sped off, laughing, into the waiting night.

Chiaroscuro

WHEN I WAS seven, my friend Sol was hit by lightning and died. He was on a rooftop quietly playing marbles when this happened. Burnt to cinders, we were told by the neighborhood gossips. He'd caught fire, we were assured, but never felt a thing. I only remember a frenzy of ambulances and long clean sirens cleaving the silence of that damp October night. Later, my father came to sit with me. This happens to one in several millions, he said, as if knowledge of the bare statistics mitigated the horror. He was trying to help, I think. Or perhaps he believed I thought it would happen to me. Until now, Sol and I had shared everything—secrets, chocolates, friends, even a birth date. We would marry at eighteen, we promised each other, and move to a magical world beyond the seas, to London or New York or Timbuktu. We'd have six children, two cows, and a heart-shaped tattoo with "Eternally Yours" sketched on our behinds. But now Sol was somewhere else, and I was seven years old and under the covers in my bed counting spots before my eyes in the darkness.

After that I cleared out my play closet. Out went my collection of teddy bears and picture books. In its place was an emptiness, the oak panels reflecting their own wood shine. The space I made seemed almost holy, though Mother thought my efforts a waste. An empty cupboard is no better than an empty cup, she said in a cryptic aside.

Mother always filled things up—cups, water jugs, vases, boxes, arms—
as if color and weight equaled a superior quality of life. Mother never
understood that this was my dreamtime place. Here I could hide,
slide the doors shut behind me, scrunch my eyes tight, and breathe in
another world. When I opened my eyes, the glow from the closet's
lone bulb seemed to set the polished walls shimmering, and I could
feel what Sol must have felt: dazzle and darkness. I was sharing this
with him, as always. He would know, wherever he was, that I knew
what he knew, saw what he had seen. But to Mother I only said that
I was tired of teddy bears and picture books. What she thought I
couldn't tell, but she stirred the soup pot vigorously.

One in millions. I said this to myself many times, as if the key, the
answer to it all, lay there. The phrase was heavy on my lips, stubbornly
resistant to knowledge. Sometimes I said the words out of context to
see if by deflection, some quirk of physics, the meaning would suddenly come to me. Thanks for the beans, Mother, I said to her at lunch,
you're one in millions. Mother looked at me oddly, pursed her lips,
and offered me more rice. At the Doon Club tennis courts, when
Father served a clean ace to win the Retired Wallahs Rotating Cup, I
pointed out that he was one in a million. Oh, the *serve* was one in a
million, Father protested modestly. But he seemed pleased. Still, this
wasn't what I was looking for, and in time the phrase slipped away
from me, lost its magic urgency, became as bland as "Pass the salt" or
"Is the bath water hot?" If Sol was one in a million, I was one among
far less—a dozen, say. He was chosen. I was ordinary. He had been
touched and transformed by forces I didn't understand. I was left
cleaning out the closet. There was one way to bridge the chasm, to
bring Sol back to life, but I would wait to try it until the most magical
of moments. I would wait until the moment was so right and shimmering that Sol would have to come back. This was my weapon that
nobody knew of, not even Mother, even though she had pursed her
lips at the beans. This was between Sol and me.

The winter had almost guttered into spring when Father was ill.
One February morning he sat in his chair, ashen as the cinders in the

grate. Then his fingers splayed out in front of him, his mouth working, he heaved and fell. It all happened suddenly, so cleanly, as if rehearsed and perfected for weeks. Again the sirens, the screech of wheels, the white coats in perpetual motion. Heart seizures weren't one in a million. But they deprived you just the same, darkness but no dazzle, and a long waiting.

Now I knew there was no turning back. This was the moment. I had to do it without delay; there was no time to waste. While they carried Father out, I rushed into the closet, scrunched my eyes tight, opened them in the shimmer, and called out: "Sol! Sol! Sol!" I wanted to keep my mind blank, like death must be, but Father and Sol gusted in and out in confusing pictures. Leaves in a storm and I the calm axis. Here was Father playing marbles on a roof. Here was Sol serving ace after ace. Here was Father with two cows. Here was Sol hunched over the breakfast table. The pictures eddied and rushed. The more frantic they grew, the clearer my voice became, tolling like a bell: "Sol! Sol! Sol!" The closet rang with voices, some mine, some echoes, some from what seemed another place—where Sol was, maybe. The closet seemed to groan and reverberate, as if shaken by lightning and thunder. Any minute now it would burst open and I would find myself in a green valley fed by limpid brooks and red with hibiscus. I would run through tall grass and, wading into the waters, see Sol picking flowers. I would open my eyes and he'd be there, hibiscus-laden, laughing. Where have you been, Talina? he'd say, as if it were I who had burned, falling in ashes. I was filled to bursting with a certainty so strong it seemed a celebration almost. Sobbing, I opened my eyes. The bulb winked at the walls.

I fell asleep, I think, because I awoke to a deeper darkness. It was late, much past my bedtime. Slowly I crawled out of the closet, my tongue furred, my feet heavy. My mind felt like lead. Then I heard my name. Mother was in her chair by the window, knitting without pause, her fingers deft, her body defined by a thin ray of moonlight. Your father will be well, she said quietly, and he will be home soon. The shaft of light in which she sat so motionless was like the light that would have touched Sol if he'd been lucky; if he had been like one of us, one in a dozen, or less. This light fell in a benediction, caressing Mother, slipping gently over my father in his hospital bed six streets away. I reached out and stroked my mother's arm. It was warm like bath water, her skin the texture of hibiscus.

We stayed together for some time, my mother and I, invaded only by small night sounds and the raspy whirr of crickets. Then I stood up and turned to return to my room. Mother looked at me quizzically. Are you all right? I told her I was fine, that I had some cleaning up to do. Then I went to my closet and stacked it up again with teddy bears and picture books.

Some years later we moved to a house at the edge of town, an old army bungalow surrounded by the rise of the Siwalik Hills. The summer I turned sixteen, I got lost in the thick woods there. They weren't that deep—about three miles at the most. All I had to do was cycle for all I was worth, and in minutes I'd be on the dirt road leading into town. But a stir in the leaves gave me pause.

I dismounted and stood listening. Branches arched like claws overhead. The sky crawled on a white belly of clouds. Shadows fell in tessellated patterns of gray and black. There was a faint thrumming all around, as if the air were being strung and practised for an overture. And yet there was nothing, just a silence of moving shadows, a bulb winking at the walls. I remembered Sol, of whom I hadn't thought in years. And foolishly again I waited, not for answers but simply for an end to the terror the woods were building in me, chord by chord, like dissonant music. When the cacophony grew too much to bear, I remounted and pedaled furiously, banshees screaming past my ears, my feet assuming a clockwork of their own. The pathless ground threw up leaves and stones, swirls of dust rose and settled. The air was cool and steady as I hurled myself into the falling light.

Isfahan Is Half the World

TWO TOWERS, A purple banana, a linen shirt, a clock without a face, a woman at a ticket window, a plane, all of which together could make up a Dali painting but not a history.

You can pack a bag, fill it up with wonder and clean underwear, why not, it's in the scheme of things. If schemes were things, which they are not. Schemes, like history, are broken stories, full of what-ifs and almosts. Schema: *a representation of a plan or theory in the form of an outline or model.* In Kantian philosophy: *a conception of what is common to all members of a class; a general or essential type or form.* Travel is schemata, models of possibility; travelers, a conception of belonging within a type. A type that doesn't belong, even in theory. I scheme, you scheme, we all . . . But ice cream melts. Like models and hopes of belonging. Instead you scrabble in the dust and kiss the earth. This is where your feet are now.

I got off the British Airways plane in New York in September 2002, still eating that rancid banana, all crumpled in my linen shirt and jeans, a smashed travel clock in my luggage (though I wasn't to know of this until the unpacking, the disordered unpacking, in an airport hotel room). There was a woman at the subway ticket booth, scowling. She didn't welcome me to America. She said, "You can't eat here," though she didn't explain the reason why.

I am a painting in that moment, without history. A set of daubs and squiggles on a subway canvas. Arrival is an art of its own unmaking.

A tower, not part of schemata. Out of the blue, literally. But in itself, a thing alone, a history of the moment in its blaze of light.

By the time I stepped off that plane, NineEleven was already a single word. A word so full of its own weight it sank into silence as it was spoken. This was not always the way it was seen elsewhere. Back in India the word was lighter, fiery, prone to combustion. A word that implied that the fate of the world was both immediate and distant, like overhanging scaffolding on a broken beam. From afar, the word held mystery and threat; in America it was a keening. To me, the word meant the impolite ticket-booth woman, swaths of black and white and brown faces pretending they were part of the crowds, just people with suitcases and a place to go.

And behind it all, chaos and sorrow, but of a kind cinematic, in a blurred and parallel realm. *Time* magazine covers of somber men, and more immediately a sharp-eyed customs man: "What's in your bag, ma'am?" And the meekness of my response. Just papers, money, a passport, cosmetics, a clock. No perfume bottles, no cologne. "You can move on." SevenEleven had been the word once in parlance. Uncles, family friends, the gardener's affluent brother-in-law. They were SevenEleven men, each with a convenience store in New Jersey or Indiana and an additional bank account in Mumbai, Calcutta, Pune. People who traded candy bars and toiletries over counters to strangers with change and cars growling in the lot, motor running. SevenEleven was the gateway to America. NineEleven shut the door.

Or that was the story I was told. Be very careful. Sikhs have been killed for wearing turbans. A man in jail for spelling his name out loud: "T for Terrorist, E for Ebrahim, K for Kalashnikov . . ." He thought his high jinks made him appealing to the airport authorities. He was from Ludhiana. Guantánamo sounded like a gecko or a Mexican song. Not so, he found out, the wrong way. He was the cautionary tale: you will be seen as someone else, it's the times, nobody's fault. Watch your step, be a good girl, visit Disney World, get a mortgage. A husband, maybe, but not necessarily. There are suitable options here as well.

My parents waved me off at the New Delhi airport, then moved again, to Ooty, after my father tired of northern India and found a small brick home up in the Nilgiris from where they could see tea plantations tumble down the hills through blue-lit mists. In the mornings they arose to quiet cups of tea and the newspapers. My childhood was their photo album, leafed through in moments, set aside. That was the past, and they were too contained for nostalgia. The present was what they sought, in walks around the tea plantations, in get-togethers with other retirees. The world came in through narratives from which they stayed remote. But yet narratives became their mode of connection and concern. Letters flew across the seas. Emails morphed into ceaseless counsel. Remember to work hard. Be watchful. Sikh men, Guantánamo. Be safe. Visit old friends, in Indiana, Pennsylvania, California. Nina, Anu, Maitreya. Maybe Siddharth, a nice fellow, really. Don't listen to gossip. Keep those contacts intact, you never know when you'll need a helping hand, or, even better, be one. Be strong, successful. Make us proud.

I left them lonely, waving goodbye with a red checkered scarf before boarding the airplane, armed with the promise of a graduate fellowship at Syracuse, two hundred dollars, luggage, and a list of to-do's.

Here was my list, my private conception for belonging:

Baywatch
McDonald's
Macy's
The Mall of America
Baseball (and why it was not cricket)
Cartoon character fuzzy house slippers
Pineapple pizza
Crime (but not directly)
Everything in Washington DC

The United Nations
Dustin Hoffman
God (the American version, in good clothing)

I can't say I had much success with the list apart from the pizza and McDonald's, neither of which required effort but could be brought to your door or requested over a squawky receptor. *Baywatch* was no longer playing, and the slippers gave me a sense of squashing things underfoot. And meeting God in your Sunday best was disconcerting, rather like an appointment with a criminal defense lawyer who barely believed your protestations but felt obliged to anyway. Dustin Hoffman had grown old.

So it's fair to say that my America didn't quite work out as planned. Except for work at graduate school and the friends who were inevitable in a crowded dorm.

What sort of Indian name is Talina? demanded James, my dorm-room neighbor. Is it Sanskrit? He was told all Indian names have origins in mythology, trailing weights of impossible expectation. He'd heard of Sanjay Gupta and Pico Iyer. Maybe a Raj or two, a Kumar and a Patel. The likes of Amartya Sen and Sundar Pichai were still down the road.

Not very, I admitted. Sort of made up. My father wanted to upend the status quo.

That made no sense but sounded pretty important.

News to me, said James cheerfully, and didn't challenge the information. He was a Sunday-best sort of fellow, live and let live if you weren't the same. All God's children. He offered me half of his lunch sandwich, and a year later a diamond ring.

I think sometimes of that man from Ludhiana. I give him a history and a future. I fill in gaps and add flourishes. His is my other story. So he comes from a village where the Green Revolution was in bloom until the subsidies grew scarcer, the competition greater. He couldn't compete against the agribusiness conglomerates that became a byword in Indian economic restructuring in the nineties. He decided to take his

95

chances with a brother-in-law in New York who ran his own taxi service. The man from Ludhiana applied for the immigration lottery; he was chosen. What happens next is anybody's guess. Perhaps he moved in with his sister and brother-in-law after the stint in jail and a host of warnings from the local police. He bought a taxi, then three more, with help from the brother-in-law. He developed a side business in imported spices. He married a woman from the Bronx, and they had two bonny children, a boy and a girl. He bought a house in Queens, two bedrooms and a tiny porch out front. He learned to barbecue pork ribs and flew the Stars and Stripes outside his door to allay the suspicions of neighbors, and so his turban would become a sign of melting-pot solidarity, not a threat. All his neighbors thought so too. They agreed he was one of the good ones. His son was partial to the Knicks; his daughter became a popular high school cheerleader. They all lived happily ever after.

Or not.

Perhaps he stayed in jail. Perhaps the authorities found probable cause for terroristic intentions. Perhaps he was deported.

Or perhaps, as neither extreme seems likely, he found work as a part-time doorman on the Upper East Side where beautiful women breezed past him, through the shimmering glass doors, through the shining foyer, up the speedy elevator, into a different ether. He smiled and learned the tricks of murmured compliance—"Good morning, sir (or madam), what a beautiful day it is today!" He softened his growling consonants to please the American ear. He was the right sort of immigrant, grateful and upbeat. One day, the beautiful women said to each other on their way to the elevator, he will have a fleet of taxis! Such a charming man.

I try out written drafts of all three versions.

I show James my Ludhiana-man stories, but he is unimpressed, even bored. Not very good, he says, not unkindly and in his best courtly manner. Just another immigrant story. Full of clichés, really.

My own story loops an easy arc from A to Z without much drama in between. The in-between is baskets of unwashed laundry, trips to assorted Greek islands in the summers, chicken biryani recipes, an unfortunate encounter with a drunken sailor on a Chicago bus, two job offers, a near-cancer scare, and a beat-up Toyota. The stuff of life, really. Belonging within the type. Nothing that resets a broken clock.

I married James and never regretted it. We are older now, and other than an unexpected affair in midlife, James has remained a good partner. Our marriage is an agreeable constant. We smile at each other over breakfast cups of coffee. We reach out our hands at Christmas and give thanks for our blessings. We send Christmas cards to everyone we know, even people we meet briefly on vacations. We celebrate birthdays and anniversaries with cake and fervent declarations. We live without distress. Our ranch-style house in Eau Claire has a flowing yard with red geraniums in a pot outside the front door. A blue-and-white-striped awning over the deck. A barbecue with room for five steaks and a single row of potatoes. We hang an Etsy sign on our front door that says:

IN THIS HOUSE, WE BELIEVE:
BLACK LIVES MATTER
WOMEN'S RIGHTS ARE HUMAN RIGHTS
NO HUMAN IS ILLEGAL
LOVE IS LOVE
SCIENCE IS REAL
KINDNESS IS EVERYTHING

We see these signs spring up everywhere on immaculate front lawns.

We tell ourselves we are good people.

We agree we are one among millions. Nothing more, or less.

When Minneapolis was burning (yes, one among many cities), I thought of SevenEleven. Not the falling towers but the frightened men huddled in their corner shops, waiting for ICE or the police to beat them out of hiding. People with mounds of basmati rice to sell, and mango pickles on a shelf. Mosques emptied and hearts in quarantine.

My man from Ludhiana has become a ghostly presence on the borders of the city. He will not go away.

We are all now writing stories. Sometimes in memory, sometimes in air. The wind lifts and passes us in gusts. Our stories scatter over continents, camouflaged histories we cannot share. We await the apocalypse, or at least a bloodless street and a safe vaccine.

Our words tell us we will survive. Our fingers knit and purl, purl and knit. The towers fall, and they are falling still.

Triptych, with Interruptions

1

Inside my house the air is still. I have imagined a place for myself, a quiet room where no birds fly, where children's voices are a memory, where the squatting inkwell is a point of steady reference in a present of lightweight ballpoint pens. But my room is a compromised solitude. I do not have five hundred pounds. I make pennies to my husband's paycheck. I cook and clean, I smile and inveigh against the weight of the world. I have become the cliché I once despised, the woman whose only mystique is that she is mortal.

But I have imagined a room of my own, even if it is invaded sometimes by recipes and bills, sometimes a ringing phone, sometimes an inward collapse of the will. All these things are the stuff of poetry for more attuned selves; to me, they cross boundaries and set up flags. They must be dismantled, shooed away. In their place another life arises. The room becomes a foundry. Little flames rise and fall. A whole sun shines in for a moment. The dark covers the furniture. Nothing goes as required by the clock.

And so, a story. Some of it is true. Mostly it is lies.

I'll decide, says the Angel in the House, tapping her dainty foot. Let memory tell the story. *Above all, be pure.*

Memory won't speak. Instead it dances, hides, capers, and makes a fool of me. It covers where it should reveal. Sometimes it throws the whole bag at my feet—figure that out, it says. The memory keeper is an American; ten years in this new country has given it a new vocabulary and bearing. It is supremely confident and has excellent self-esteem, but every now and then the immigrant's voice falters through. My memory keeper is a fraud.

And so, where to begin? Hosha. Narrator. Room. Walk. Return. A journey motif without the requisite huzzahs. The people are all changed, their spirit preserved like some enduring jelly.

Say, 'like a Twinkie,' suggests the memory keeper. They pretty much last forever.

I push it off the table.

The storyteller's journey is my story and is not. One day I came to America with a bag, two hundred dollars (not quite five hundred pounds, so we're circling the room), and a magic key. The fellowship to a university opened doors, but the palace of enchanted wonders was too vast, technicolored in technology and in ambitions that surpassed my own. I had an inkwell in the land of shiny ballpoint hopes, a feathered pen where a computer was a password.

Hosha, muses my memory keeper, undeterred. Make him six feet tall. Give him a head of yellow hair, like a haystack or the morning sun. Or at least a cheerful lightbulb.

Be nice, adds the Angel. Give him a Sad Past and a Kindly Disposition.

Quiet, I command.

(The memory keeper and the Angel are canoodling. This cannot bode well.)

The world is full of all sorts of people. . . .

2

The world is full of all sorts of people. This astonishing fact comes to me one Sunday while I am peeling peaches (such as they are, fuzzy and overripe to the touch) over the kitchen counter, my freshly washed hair neatly turbaned into a peach-mimicking fuzz of Egyptian toweling. The thought bedazzles, demands to be shared in my delight-befogged moment of wonder. So I say it aloud carefully but with passion, savoring the sweet, rounded syllables like fruit.

"What?" asks Hosha, blind without his glasses, unwindowed as a wall.

I repeat the epiphany in dulcet octaves so he might be modulated into its recognition.

"Bloody cliché," snorts Hosha. He's given to bad temper in the mornings, even though now the sun is streaming in with an eleven o'clock glare. Some people are just like that, and it takes an internet romance or a lottery windfall to change their gears.

"You're not a good person," I say to him, having watched Dr. Phil till all hours. "You need help."

"You—walking cliché," he mutters in reply, suspicious of complete sentences before a full repast.

"Walking cliché? The walking part of it is a cliché in itself," I say. "As in 'walking encyclopedia' or 'walking stick.'"

Not entirely true, of course, that part about the stick, because a stick is a thing. Things can be clichés, like my Malibu Barbie or lawn signs that still say "The Change We Need," though it's four years later and the second inauguration has thrown its hat and balloons in the air. Clichés aside, the point is for Hosha to button up because it is rude to bat away my attempts at good nutrition and convivial repartee. Hosha glares halfheartedly, squinting through the neon sunlight at what he thinks is me but is instead the new umbrella stand shooting off silver spikes like fireworks.

Mildly annoyed by the comparison, I feel the need to retaliate.

"Sour kraut," I say, though in a friendly way because of good manners and the high road.

"Cabbagehead," murmurs Hosha dreamily, as if composing a sonnet. He reflects for a moment, weighing some connection between the words—"sour kraut," "cabbagehead"—but that is just the English teacher in him idly kicking sand in the desert. I whip off my towel-turban and shake my hair loose, as is seemly for impending battle, much like the stamping of hooves or the twirling of gauntlets. But Hosha assumes his defeated owl expression, which can only mean one thing.

"WhereAreMuhGlasses?" asks Hosha.

This isn't his real name, as you must have guessed. His name is Heinrich, a legacy handed down from his Nazi grandfather, the grumpy one who wore a red fedora to bed. "How did you get this name, Hosha?" people inquire, and always he gives them the same reply. When he was a baby two months old, his parents awakened to a thunderous sound. Their baby had sneezed beyond all proportion to his weight and age. Like a lightning bolt—HOOOr-sha! At that pivotal moment his mother rechristened him, certain the sneeze had been fashioned by the Hand of God. Commendable, I think, to follow this train of thought. I once had a geography teacher, Mrs. Ramprasad, who named her newborn Rover after a beloved long-gone pet. Not surprisingly, Rover Ramprasad grew up taking cover at the sight of a feline whisker. On balance, a vigilant approach to cats is preferable to being named after a bodily function for which there is no defensive recourse.

"WhereAreMuhBloodyGlasses?" demands Hosha, the big post-sneeze baby, rattling his crib.

Hosha spent the first fourteen years of his life in England, where the word "bloody," as described in the handy guidebook *Interpreting British English for the Foreign Ear*, indicates an extreme form of frustration or sophistication, as in "bloody hell" or "bloody good show, old chum." This latter example is open to debate because "bloody good show" has shown some wear, now used mostly by postcolonials eager to prove their affinity with upper-class Brits who are mostly dead.

"Off to get the paper," I say to Hosha, without rancor, as is my temperament.

I don't expect a reply, nor do I get one. Hosha has recovered his glasses from the sideboard and is now shaping his fingernails with my scalloped-handled mother-of-pearl pocketknife. He splays out his fingers like crippled spiders walking in the air. Such efforts at arm-chair yoga, he contends, improve his concentration.

A strange man in need of help, though it must be admitted that is part of Hosha's charm. (The other part is that he can pay the bills, which is to me an attraction as comforting as the Statue of Liberty to a shipwrecked immigrant, since I am an out-of-work English teacher.)

"Get lunch," calls Hosha, waving the knife at the closing door. Too late, too late, I am down the stairs and into the open on a late Sunday morning, in search of the newspaper and different people, and the change, at least for now, I need.

Outside, the weather is balmy. I tread lightly over potholes and con-crete, my feet tripping a careless dance to the tune of *one-hup, two-hup, tweedle-hup, whee,* which even in the kindest of interpretations is not music. On the other hand, the notes provide a cantata for my feet so I can hoist and step, step, and kick, without much attention from the crowds who think me physically deficient. I accept the sym-pathy of a warm glance or the diplomacy of an averted one with the same carelessness.

Onehuptwo. I am six years old and in a garden in spring.

There are things to be seen and not seen on the street. Not to be seen is a man in a shiny limo hoisting both feet through the door, ready to spring the world into action. To be seen is a rambunctious dog on a leash leading a middle-aged woman straight into a bush. If the arrangement were up to me, she'd be in the car with the dog, the two of them sipping champagne while the man (fiftyish, with a crew-cut and pepper goatee, black briefcase in hand) might end up twirling around on his head for the pleasure of the passersby.

"Life is not for arranging," says Hosha in his more tempered moments. Full of wise saws is Hosha. Life arranges us, and we are the displays. We pose and freeze. Once he wrote an essay on fate and the many ways it tricks us into beautiful paralysis. Utter stillness like a vase. His professor was unsympathetic. "Pretentious," she wrote on the bottom of the last page. "And borrowed from Keats." That was her only comment. Hosha took the comment personally as retaliation for having earlier mentioned his grandfather in a graduate seminar on Holocaust literature. The professor was Jewish.

"She means an urn," explained Hosha. "An urn is different," he said, shaking his head in disappointment. "A thing you fill with ashes and set discreetly but meaningfully upon your mantelpiece. A vase is for life, for water and flowers." Completely at odds.

Once a mouse fell into Hosha's sock drawer and chewed up his blue linen underpants. Hosha lifted out the mouse, gave it a wedge of cheese, and set it free in the communal basement laundry room. Though this simple gesture was not appreciated by other brownstone occupants, especially those availing themselves of the machines at that particular time, the mouse did not reappear in the sock drawer, laundry room, or anywhere else we imagined. Mollified by cheese, the mouse left us alone. I demur, but only mildly. Hosha's point is that the professor was given a slice of poisoned cheese and spat it right back out at him. He sees justice in this act and a reaffirming of the causal nature of the universe. Still, he blacked out the professor's remark, gave himself an A, and wrote "Excellent!" after it. Whatever our understanding of the moral immensity of our actions, we all have a reputation to consider.

In my garden in Dehradun I am almost eight, and my birthday looms ahead like a red balloon. Run! Get it! cries my father, as I chase a butterfly three days before an uncle dies in a boating accident. On my birthday the air is somber, full of mourning ghosts who turn out to be aged relatives at the funeral. As good as ghosts, for I never see them again, only hear of their passings like wind shifts over water. One early next year, another in late fall, all strung out like a line of paper cutouts. I count my years by their demise, shedding my childhood with their losses.

Now, years later, my parents are gone too, drifting like whispers into the ether. My birthdays range the sky in search of them, balloons and ghosts, untethered.

I am closing in on the newsstand, where people of all color and manner of clothing are buying magazines. A young man with a diamond nose-ring is counting his change loudly as if to impress an audience. An old woman is gazing sleepily at a cover photograph of a young woman with a four-year-old child latched to her left breast. There are no magazines with bold pictures of bloodied soldiers in the desert. A Vietnamese man with black-edged glasses and a three-piece suit is handing over money for a copy of *Vogue*. I'd have guessed the *Wall Street Journal*, but what do I know? I live with Hosha, and the ghosts of my relatives and his Nazi fedora-hatted grandfather fill our home with remorse. We speak of them desultorily, our guilt separate, mine smudgy with filial omissions, his fat and glutinous with shame.

Three blocks away the clouds merge slightly.

"Rain?" inquires Hosha when the silence in rooms gets too long. Other people cough or just get up and leave. I am a leaver. Of rooms, of love and dogs, of unmourned kin. I walk into bushes and recover. I do not enter limousines, even in dreams. I am a foot soldier, one foot out at a time. I rarely check the sky and only for wildly morphing clouds, signs of sleet, snow, the unexpected. Hosha is a great one for the weather. Daily forecasts keep him in touch with the world outside, and he relays them to the walls, to me.

"Not much difference in the audience," says Hosha. "At least the walls are nicely painted."

I am glad not to be a painted woman. I have small feet, arthritic fingers, and a head of shiny brown hair. My nose is sharp, and my chin pointed. I could be a weathervane leaning into the wind if the Fates had so decreed. Perhaps I already am, one in my second-floor apartment with Hosha, testing my life with each drift of rain.

In my Dehradun garden were twelve stunted lichee trees, randomly planted. You had to tread cautiously if you had a dog on a leash. Dogs would run everywhere, a consternation underfoot. You, on the other hand, had to steer clear of branches so low they almost touched your hands. They held on to you, gnarled fingers reaching. Perhaps they saw affinity in my fingers. Wood and bone.

On the street here are no lichee trees. Sometimes a patch of grass, sometimes a bush, once a bush with a woman in it. No lichee trees.

Before I left for America, my mother gave me a beautiful pearl-handled penknife, perhaps to show me that lovers and strangers must be kept at bay. On my first attempt at dormitory cooking, I sliced my index finger almost all the way off with this knife.

The University Hospital nurse thought I was a fool. Only immigrants slice tomatoes with such heedless heft.

The street at noon is temperamental. Sometimes it empties quickly as if a flying saucer were spitting beams of destruction from up on high; other times it fills like a jug about to overflow with honks and screeches. Right now, it overflows. I can't cross the street to the news-stand because the traffic is mad dogs on the loose. Lunchtime, and the restaurants in the square are filling their bellies with hungry Sunday walkers.

Hosha's sadstory is not his story at all. He appropriated it because it gave him cover.

"When I was thirteen"—fourteen, twelve, he changes dates—"we lived in London." This part is always the same and full of foreboding. "We lived just off the East End in a grimy row of flats, in a three-room apartment, really a clump of interconnected bedsits, because that's all the rent my father could afford." I always look sympathetic. Truly, who can live surrounded by walls and little streets with no way out especially if you are an immigrant displaced by the War with no money and English that gutters down people's ears in spits and gargles?

"One day," says Hosha, "while we were looking out of our living room window onto the alley behind the burned-out theater, we saw a woman sitting squarely on a man."

"Impossible!" I cry, for such a response is required to embellish the moment.

"I was looking out of the window with my mother and baby sister"—who died of meningitis, but that story was told only once— "when my father coming homewards from his job as an assistant shop manager began gesticulating oddly from the street. At first, I thought he was having a heart attack or possibly readying for song as he did so often while in public places in Germany—my father, my ham—but he was drawing our attention to a very large woman sitting atop a very small man at the L-turn in the alleyway. Some might see this moment as crude or sexual in nature, but if you were there, you could tell it was neither. She had her skirts spread over him so all you could see was his white face with a ginger moustache under a mountain of gingham, and he said in tones that carried clearly across to us, 'You're my man, Joanna.' And she said, 'I would never doubt that, Horace.'

"At this point," says Hosha, "my mother, my sister, and I shut the window and did not look out again, but we remembered that moment for its sheer beauty."

"It's not *your* story," I say, jealous. "It belongs to Horace."

"I made it up," says Hosha. "Not the story but the moment, and it kept me alive through grammar school. Sometimes even now I close my eyes and think of what it must be to be the woman, the man, or both of them at once, so random and fisted in a heap."

Of all his England stories, this is the one he likes to tell. I want to hear the Loss-of-Sister story, the Parents-Retired-in-Devon story, the First-Love-Was-an-Italian Girl story, the Coming-to-America-Without-Funds story. The Meeting-Me story. I wonder if they don't touch him anymore or hold him too closely. I think you're lying, I say, because you won't tell the other stories, but Hosha shakes his great head with yellow hair as if to say, you know nothing. That much is true, I must admit. Hosha is six feet tall. He speaks German and English. He has a PhD in Restoration drama and a job at a community college. We met at a farmer's market reaching for the same tomato. We were hungry in indeterminate ways. We both needed help.

"Tell me about your little sister," I said to him once late at night when he was almost asleep and susceptible to confession.

"When she was three," said Hosha on cue, as if talking to the walls, "she fell ill. I was babysitting, looking out of the window at a tree full of strong branches, when her fever went up and she gave a cry. Like the mewling of an alley kitten. The trees outside looked like prizefighters, arms uplifted in the air. I thought it might rain. As I watched the clouds and waited for my mother to return with the doctor, my sister died. I was holding her in my arms, but I couldn't help her. She was everything to me, but she was gone."

Then, because he had told me a story with an ending, Hosha arose abruptly to brush his teeth. It seemed to add up, even when I held out my arms and he ignored me.

My stories don't add up much at all; they have beginnings, middles, and ends. Some have morals or at least recommendations. If we all love one another, we can be happy. When climbing trees, don't miss a branch to show off or you'll need antiseptic liquid on a cotton ball. Neighborhood picnics can bring the community together. My stories have a big white house at the center and a happy, singing father and a mother who made omelets at two in the morning if you so desired. My stories discuss birthday parties, trips to the Vale of Kashmir, and secret clubhouses. My stories are spiced with words like *pavadai*, *shehnai*, *gulmohor*, and *ghazal*. The exotica dazzle me but leave Hosha cold. This is depressing because I need to see my exotic past through his eyes to fully appreciate such splendor; otherwise it's all just clothes and flowers and music, much as anywhere.

"You're a reverse Orientalist," says Hosha, when what I just wish to do is experience myself as a creature of the local imagination.

I cook him matar masala, dosa sambar, and vadai.

"Just like my mother made in Bavaria!" cries Hosha, and indeed he believes this observation, having reworked his past into pastiche.

Tell me your happystory, demands Hosha.
    I've come to a new and alien country, I say.
    Your sadstory?
    It's about the same.
    You're either a total liar or completely truthful, muses Hosha.
    I am pleased to be a total-complete, much better than halves and partly.

But, of course, there is a story. We all have stories. Sometimes neither happy nor sad but merely there like a stone or a feather that will hold you down with its lightly impervious filters.
    My story is when time stopped for just a moment with a knock at the door. In Dehradun, 1977.
    Was it a dark and stormy night? inquires Hosha, hands clasped, all excited.
    It was a balmy spring morning, I tell him.
    He is disappointed but listens politely.
    A furious knocking at the door. Five a.m. or so. "Darwaaza kholo! O-pun the doh!" Indira Amma calling, by proxy, her henchmen armed with sticks. Her henchmen shouting loudly, "Indira Gandhi Zindabad!" My father groggy and confused, his hand on the door-knob, half lit in the waning dark. "Who is it?" asks my mother, fearful, her fingers knotted. I am awake, alert, all that noise drowning out the birds in their matins. "Indira Amma calling," says my father over his shoulder, never one to lose irony, as the pounding on the door gets louder, the shouting louder.
    "Singhania-ji, darwaaz kohl de! Darwaaza kholo!"
    Singhania is our neighbor, the one in the Congress Party who defected. Who has not since been heard from or seen.
    "Whozzit?" repeats my mother.

But my father does not hear her. He opens the door, trusting as a mole.

A crowd of men reach in for him. Then a pause, a slur. "Sala! Ye tho nahi hai Singhania!" Not Singhania, after all. A man in a purple turban shoves my father against the door. He rests against the door, limp as my Raggedy Ann doll but not smiling like her in perpetual delight. He is instead mute, impassive. He is waiting for the call. The men raise their sticks, their mission interrupted. How quickly the sticks rise and fall, how swiftly my father falls.

So lucky, say our friends later in the day (that we were not Singhania). So lucky (that we were not defectors). So lucky (that the goons were bent on blood, just not yours). So lucky. Lucky, lucky us.

Did this really happen? inquires Hosha. Did it happen, or did you dream it? You were five years old.

I could have dreamed it. I could have made it up. If Singhania hadn't disappeared for good. Jail cell, said the papers. Torture. In the short term. In the long term? Retirement in Ooty, said the local Congressman, smiling kindly. Singhania was very tired and needed to rest. (Under the sod, we later heard, but why sully a bright moment?) Then the prime minister called it all off, held elections. And everybody loved her all over again until she died in a hail of bullets, and the UnEmergency became a footnote in the annals, something for historians and novelists to ponder and bemoan.

You cannot remember things from when you were five, says Hosha, competitive even in trauma. What can a stick-wielding goon hold against a sleepy Nazi? Only the brunt of memory, each sharper for the frightened one. Each removed for the listener, each softened by the storyteller, cushioned by metaphor and healing.

Oh, sorry, I say, smacking my head. It happened yesterday! I was forty-two, not five. And it wasn't Indiraji's henchmen, it was Modi's! And my father didn't open the door, *I* did, in a blue and silver sari (which was sartorially at odds with the orange-clad acolytes, but tastes differ), I opened the door, and there they were, just the same as before, lathis up and glowering—

Liar, says Hosha. He is losing patience.

You open up the door, and there's a world, just like this one, only in a convulsive universe. One that repeats itself, over and over, till your head is whirling with its memories and your heart is on a pike.

And so the story has no ending. It loops and loops. An aberration in my telling.

Even if true, which I doubt, says Hosha, remember we are not refugees. We are not *fleeing from* or *running toward*. Our ethos is transitional but not ravaged. Our bloodletting is memory, our hands remain unmarked. We are the margins of our histories, the ones who walk a fine line vanishing even as we lift our feet, nomads of the air. We leave no trace.

That evening we had a picnic, I say to Hosha, to cheer him up. My mother made omelets and matar masala.

You are such a liar, muses Hosha. Your voice is real and believable, but the facts are not.

I take bits of life and let them wander on a narrative.

Like ants crawling on a stick, suggests Hosha.

Not a compliment entirely.

In a stroller ahead is a fat baby waving a rattle that sings "The Wheels on the Bus." Her young mother seems slightly askew with bouncing the stroller over sloping grassy mounds in Rittenhouse Square Park. We have no children, because Hosha has A Problem, the nature of which we don't discuss. It has to do with liquid in a test tube and much sad shaking of the head. "Sorry, sorry," says the doctor. "I'll be back." And he is, in a minute, with printed forms and hope, but I cut my losses. We'll adopt, we promise the doctor, but we don't. In our brownstone, it's all we can do to swat away the clichés. There's no time now for children.

The baby considers me with thoughtful eyes.

"Lovely little package," my mother would say.

The baby chews on the tassels of her white cap with embroidered strawberries.

Strawberries are like lichees, fat red teardrops, the blood on my index finger that flowed onto the nurse's white uniform.

"Stupid immigrant," she had said.

Or perhaps not. Maybe it was "stupid implement," meaning the knife. I didn't ask her to repeat it.

"Arab terrorist," the nurse said, swabbing at my open hand.

"Beg pardon?" I inquired politely.

"I'd rub the wrist," she said, swabbing, swabbing. "It helps deflect the pain."

So many years later, I see the nurse through a filmy curtain of other people's blood. Whatever she said, the war now makes our language into playtime where everybody is tag. Where our language is a bloodied soldier in the desert. Where our knives stick up like rifles in the sand.

The baby watches me closely while her mother rummages through a battered black purse. Out comes a Kleenex, very orange. Hosha likes the unexpected and will appreciate this moment. The baby sneezes. On cue, the mother dives down with her Kleenex parachute, then up again. Some quick mission has been accomplished, but the baby is enraged and bawls loudly.

In the clear air I see my father swimming through the ether, trailing red balloons. *One-hup, two-hup, tweedle-hup, whee.* He is singing to the tune of the Indian national anthem. My mother floats over him like a benediction. As I wave and call to them, their forms dissolve in air.

The newsstand man sees me calling out and waving at the empty sky. He looks around as if for help or possibly the authorities.

No trees line this street. People must have branched fingers, because they lift one up to me, each the second finger. Surrounded by bent bone, I am encased in claw. I blink to clear my sight.

The baby ignores me, chortling at her pig-plump toes, while her mother says, "There now!" and smiles encouragingly at passersby. Isn't she darling?

Here is a part I must mention. I have withheld the information because it runs a nasty countercurrent against my smoothly flowing story. Not a confluence of waters here, but a confrontation. Hosha has found another love. He has said that she is Better than me. Gentler than me. (And Richer than me, though this he doesn't say.) BGR off, I think.

Soon he will be leaving. Papers, glasses, stories, and all.

The street is momentarily flying-saucer empty.

The shops have opened wide maws and swallowed everyone on the sidewalks. There's only the noonday sun, and a headache so insistent my eyes are flames.

From the curb, the baby's mother sees a small woman with lavish hair smiling at her daughter.

"No hablo español," she says sharply.

"I'm from India," I tell her. The baby laughs delightedly at the hilarity of India.

"Oh," says the mother. She turns her head to see me some other way, then gives up the effort. The information, in all, has neither pleased nor annoyed her.

"I know some people from India," she says, and we ponder this information together as if it were a nugget of pure truth.

"They're Hindu," she adds in a friendly sort of way.

"Oh," I say finally. "You know some Indian people?"

The mother has forgotten me and fusses with the diaper bag. Holding up the baby's bottle full of beige milk, she squints at it in the sunlight as if reading the mercury level on a thermometer.

I shift my attention to a more receptive audience.

"Have to go," I inform the baby in Jolly Santa tones, "to buy a newspaper."

The baby crows at the sheer joy of buying a newspaper, but her mother shakes out a pink parasol and off they go.

I give the man at the newsstand four crisp dollar notes, and he hands me the *New York Times*. "No need for change," I tell him.

"That's good to know," he says. "Most people want even a penny back."

"Oh, it takes all sorts," I tell him.

"Ain't *that* the truth!" he says. But he's looking at me strangely, as if I'm a sort beyond the all.

This is Ending One to my happystory. I have the *New York Times* under my arm. There is so much news and so much to know. I must hurry back to Hosha, who is waiting unsuccessfully for lunch, so we can discuss the war's latest events. We will sit together on a sofa and read the funnies. We will scoff at all the literary reviews, especially Hosha, who has not yet finished his great novel that will change the world. When the three o'clock sun is up riding high, we will be asleep. At five we will make dinner, and at six thirty sit down before the television to absorb the news from our favorite anchor, whose hair mimics an oiled nest. Small words will fly out of his mouth and loop between our rafters. The trees outside our windows are mighty oaks with strong-armed branches uplifted like triumphant prizefighters. Through the branches, a cool evening wind will blow, puffing its way into our little rooms. When babies or parents shake out of the leaves and float by the windows, we close the shutters, because they are so loud—and, if I might say, even rude. We live a quiet life with red strawberries for dessert and a stuffed velvet Chihuahua on the mantelpiece. Before we retire to bed, we brush our teeth with even swirls of red-and-blue-striped toothpaste.

"Think it'll rain tomorrow?" asks Hosha, scouring the sky between the branches.

"Sour kraut," I say, because I think I love him.

Then we fall asleep and lie as still as vases.

Ending Two is simpler and to the point. What happens is this. I walk up the stairs, and here in the armchair is Hosha, glasses askew, mouth wide open and snoring gently, waiting for lunch or for a miracle to change his life. No lunch, but a miracle is possible. I put down the newspaper, pick up my mother-of-pearl knife dropped by his side (so beautiful still, with scalloped handle), and run a clean sharp cross across the palm of my right hand. Up, up comes the blood tender as wisps of smoke, and when the lines fill in, I turn to Hosha and place my palm against his clueless chest. What bloodied shapes will we find when I take away my hand? A smudge in red, the shadow of a mouse, a Nazi grandfather in a red fedora, a lichee tree—and, because good things come in little packages, a sleeping baby. I have no idea. All things add up to air. But here we are in case he never wakes, my hand pressed warm against his beating heart, the scalloped knife still lovely and so latent, and sleep like love a passage through the night.

3

But I am a good girl.

The Angel hovers at my back. Choose Ending One.

They lived happily ever after.

And say, 'Like Twinkies,' commands my memory keeper. Say, 'They lived happily ever after like Twinkies.'

I lift my feathered pen.

And so of course they did.

The Gentle Cycle

THERE ARE TWO kinds of risers in the world, Maitreya believed. There are those who wake up suddenly and completely after a night's sleep and for whom the morning is an unfolding stretch of quietness tempered by the rustle of a newspaper or the light clink of spoons meeting china. Then there are those who awaken groggily, hair disheveled, their minds a stumble of half-recognized morning routines. And this lot, Maitreya thought absently, are the ones who revive smartly after a wash and tea and then begin to talk as if the night's imposed silence had retreated like the tide, leaving an empty day to be filled and filled with noise.

Maitreya was Type One, though her waking was hooded with the day's requirements hanging over her eyelids like some dreary awning. Make scrambled eggs, feed cat, wash yesterday's sweater in cool water, rearrange the kitchen cupboard crowded with soup cans. Then, all responsibility met, at least in deferred intention, Maitreya settled down to a mild and gauzy silence as she sipped her tea, read of disasters in the world, immense or private—another earthquake, distraught wives importuning husbands in newspaper advice columns. Sometimes the words wandered in seamlessly, pets lost in earthquakes, houses falling down around children's ears because a man loved his secretary with passion and his entire paycheck. One thing became the other, canceling both out, leaving Maitreya without meaningful referents to guide her, orphaned in her understanding of the world.

"This is what happens when you watch too much TV," said her brother Firoz smugly over the telephone from Arizona. Firoz radiated righteous fury, readying himself to detonate the academic world with his dissertation on failed US policies in Iran. It had to be a masterwork, having taken more than eight years.

"Eight years," sighed their father. To Maitreya it sounded as if he had said "tears." Fat, sloppy ones. Running down the sides of his face. But Firoz was never one for melodrama.

"Some things can't be hurried," Firoz pointed out to their father, and Maitreya thought this observation true and final as any edict in nature like a pregnancy or the change of seasons. Iran posed a medley of props and players, the likes of which Firoz revealed slowly, patiently, while behind this unfolding pageant sat the CIA and various US presidents with heavy tools to dismantle the scaffolding: coups, assassinations, men in dark suits, drinking Pepsi.

"East is East," said Firoz, "and the West is lost."

Lost to the culture of eternal blandishment, he meant; people knowing and bouncy, tingling with want, imitating contestants on *The Price Is Right* as they paid for groceries at the local mart, chatting with the checkout person. Not people ranging the streets, demanding homeless shelters or subsidized daycare for the working poor. An America of organized indignation was Firoz's idea of national ethos and personal achievement, and so naturally he abhorred TV with its flattering, its pandering, its puppy-dog ingratiation tugging at your beer-swilling, couch-lolling instincts. Maitreya was fearful of Firoz, not just seven years older than her, but a planet spinning in another galaxy, opinionated and removed, spewing lofty wisdom like gaseous dust. He analyzed Earth from a distance, Moses on a galactic mountain.

"I watch TV the way some men read *Playboy* for the articles," explained Firoz, "though I mean what I say."

"Oh," said Maitreya politely, wondering if more were required from her. But she was just a copywriter penning jingles on the side for an internet floral startup with lines like *Love-Power! Give Your Gal a Flower Shower Every Hour!*"

"That's what makes it a special company," Maitreya said nervously to Firoz when she ran her first jingle by him. "You know. Flowers delivered on the hour for six hours straight."

"Every hour for six hours? *Every hour?*" said Firoz in reply. "Stalker power! Ha ha! Get it?"

"Yes," said Maitreya. "That's funny."

"Would you like flowers on the dot every hour?" demanded Firoz, seeking from her a greater acknowledgement of his rightness.

"Not in the mornings," said Maitreya, still nervous and unsure of her brother, though he was her only stay, her parents no use at all, sighing deeply about invisible future grandchildren who littered their daylight hours with requests for Kool-Aid and candy canes. Television-ready children, chatting equally with grandparents and bus conductors, readied for a one-liner or a laugh.

Firoz sighed over the phone too, usually to mark the end of a conversation. His sighs were long and breathy, like someone asthmatic or in Hollywood.

"Have to go," said Firoz. "Work to do."

Me too, thought Maitreya, putting down the receiver in its cradle, then her head in her hands.

Shelter me.

Flower, power, shower. Cower. *Silly old bat.* If it rhymes, sell it.

If not, get breakfast.

"And your name is?" inquired the landlady, dry as an old wafer, six months earlier.

"Maitreya Kismet."

"Kismet? Like fate? You from I-Raq, then? One of them Arab countries?"

"India. I came here when I was nine."

The landlady looked suspicious and moved her head slightly to the left. *And?* her tilted head seemed to inquire.

"We emigrated," said Maitreya, "because my father had brothers in Detroit. He was working for an Arab oil company in Dehradun, and they sent him here. We decided to stay."

Always like this, thought Maitreya, the unfurling of my history, now on autopilot. These are the facts. This is my name. My shoes. My hair. My smiling life. And there are the truer parts I don't tell. I don't tell this: My father changed who we were, our names to notation, shorthand for arrival. Mine from Nilufer to Maitreya, the blessed one, his promise of America. Ours from Taraporevala to Kismet. His private challenge to fate. *Do what you will with me, I have you on my back. Or you can carry me.*

"Arabs? I don't accept Arabs," said the landlady, looking annoyed. "It's too much these days, what with having to think of their bombs and guns and all."

Maitreya thought this over. "Say 'Po-TAH-toes!' when irked," her father had commanded Maitreya and Firoz when they were little. A neighborhood mantra for good behavior. "Never swear, even to yourself. Say a vegetable word, one full of minerals to give you strength."

Some people actually have guns, Maitreya wanted to say but did not. My roommate Amanda in college, her boyfriend had a gun. He named it Ralph and slept next to it at night. Both were loaded, usually. One with Coors, one with menace.

Instead Maitreya smiled. The landlady surveyed her objectively. "You're a sweet little thing, MyTree," she said. "No bombs, huh? No cows, I hope, either! Cats, they're okay by me. No dogs. No dogs allowed, that's for sure. We had a pit bull once in the apartment downstairs that had to be put down after it got hold of the mailman, a black guy. Bit his pants down to wallpaper strips. I got the feeling the dog was racist. That can happen. Dogs are smart, more than pigs, though some think differently. Anyway, what I say is, if you have a dog, you have a house. Otherwise it's not fair to the dog or to mailmen, they all just get confused about things, and there's too much running around and hollerin'. You Hindu?"

"Parsi," said Maitreya.

"Pharisee? So biblical! You Christian?"

"Parsi. Zoroastrian. We came from Persia hundreds of years ago, migrating to India because of religious persecution." Once on autopilot, the words rolled freely, marbles in a line, down the slate and back again like an old bagatelle game. "We go back more than six hundred years. My ancestors are from Hyderabad."

"Is that a word?"

"It's a city in southern India."

"Sounds better than Dumptydun, or whatever," the landlady said. After a pause she added, "I always wanted to go to India. Not that I know why, what with the heat and all."

She frowned at Maitreya, a covenant of their apartness to be managed with an exchange of keys and a monthly rent check.

East is East, thought Maitreya, and West is host. She smiled back at the landlady, their smiles the high-fiving of boxers with no more urge to spar.

Maitreya got the apartment on the third floor, which suited her well. It overlooked a busy street, with a glimpse of green, a square of grass beyond the line of stores. In about forty minutes the train from the corner station took her into the center of New York City, so she could be in two worlds on the very same day—a sandwich of bustle and roar between the waking and sleeping hours.

On Saturday mornings Maitreya relaxed into her fuzzy blue Goodwill armchair, cat in lap, following her thoughts desultorily. Type One people didn't talk much, but their heads soon wandered into alleys left over from sleep. Wraiths of past acquaintances leapt up from drains, music from a kitchen radio serenaded her stumbling, a line from a punk-rock song lodged itself in a mental nook, filling the alley with din.

GUNMEUP / GUNMEDOWN / GUNMENEVER / OUTOFTOWN.

"If you have a gun," said Amanda's boyfriend one afternoon in their last year of college, "all you need is conviction."

Maitreya thought he meant of some criminal kind, but realized the misbegotten power of the word when it was rumored he had joined the Pennsylvania Militia after graduation.

"A boy from Swarthmore?" her father asked, unbelieving. "After his parents spent all that money?"

A lot was left unsaid and intended for her in that observation, as Maitreya saw it. You, who went to Swarthmore; you, who cost more than our first ranch house in Newark; you must prove you were worth the dollars—and my hours, days, months, years, a lifetime in middle-management Shell. You and Firoz must be upper management, chairmen of your own companies. You must be better than fate imagined. Carry me and your mother on your backs, our fate, our kismet.

But Firoz was a political consultant in the making, and Maitreya wrote copy for chewing gum and soap. No guns, though. Which was a start. Nobody wrote copy for guns.

"Your mind is your weapon," said their father, raising his glass to his family on his seventy-fifth birthday. "I have good ammunition in my two children!"

"Oh, po-tah-toes!" Firoz muttered, winking at Maitreya. "Po-TAH-toes with steak!"

Type One Maitreya raised her glass of milk to her parents' black-and-white wedding portrait on the living-room wall before her. How tender her mother looked, her father straight and proud in his close skullcap, his white Dreft-equivalent-washed churidar. She could see the Hyderabadi photographer moving them to the left, to the right. "Accha, Ji, ab hasna math!" No laughing now. And they obeyed, not smiling, gazing upon him sternly for posterity, now already here in a cat-scratched Jersey apartment.

Comforted, the alleyways in her head cleared suddenly with the certainty of the day ahead. She would scramble eggs, send a birthday card to Sunnu Auntie, launder sheets. Saturday again.

Soon after Maitreya moved into her new apartment, she told Firoz about her new best friend Tammy Jo. Tammy Jo who wore leather pumps and vast flowered dresses like summer tents.

"Tammy Jo?" inquired Firoz. "Does she say 'y'all' and frost her hair, does she, hmm?"

"Racist dog," said Maitreya.

"What?" asked Firoz. "Ray says what? Who's Ray?"

"Racist," said Maitreya. "Your question was racist."

"That's semantically incorrect," said Firoz. "Classist, maybe. Regionalist. Or sexist. But racist? No."

"Yes," said Maitreya.

"No," said Firoz. "Who was it mentioned Arabs? Did she say they smelled as well? Or is the poor thing scared and just needs you to take care of her?"

"We'll leave it there," said Maitreya. "I can't stand all this running around and hollerin.'"

"You are a strange sister," said Firoz, and the long sigh that followed suggested he was already aboard the spaceship, anchors aweigh, on his journey to battle the secret men in suits.

All Maitreya's old best friends from college had drifted away, smoke over the mountains, without signals, without goodbyes. Jane married an accountant and was lost in silverware and folds of drapery in Westchester. Amanda left for Montana, to fish, though for what remained unclear. And Ritu, dear Ritu, from Bombay, exchange student and fellow poet of the middling kind, went back to India and was not heard of since. Not an internet address or a LinkedIn page. And all Maitreya's letters to Ritu, seven of them, were returned from India—*addressee unknown.*

"Tammy Jo is my landlady," said Maitreya. "She thinks I'm sweet."

"That you are," said Firoz smoothly, and it was all the apology Maitreya would get.

Maitreya's internet job came to her entirely by accident while she was sitting in the park after a tedious Monday of editing an article on decaying gums for an in-house retirement community paper, *Senior's Quarterly*. There is such a thing as too much dental information, thought Maitreya, her own gums aching in sympathy, or perhaps prophecy, for all those untoothbrushed nights, soon to descend on her, she thought, like gluttonous pigeons. Peck, peck, ache, ache, drip.

"Hey," said a voice from somewhere behind her temporal lobe, so close it seemed like a rattle in her head, a sure sign of madness or molar decay.

"Me," said the voice, now attached to a man, five feet seven, with chestnut hair, a strongly tilted nose, and wire-rimmed granny glasses. "Remember me? Peter?"

Maitreya wanted to say yes, of course, wonderful to see you. She gazed at Peter, stupefied. Her gums ached. A real pigeon waddled purposefully toward her on the grass. It would fly into her mouth any moment now, if she opened it. She clutched at her brown purse as if it might be snatched.

"Oh hi," said Maitreya breathlessly, her mouth opening and shutting like a guppy.

"Peter Nowak," said the man eagerly. "Firoz's tennis partner? Remember Halloween at your place—when the cops came and shut down the party?"

Maitreya had a vague sense of parents in India, a Liberace-as-Madonna costume, streamers involving prints of gamboling sheep. And Peter Nowak following her around the sofa, saying, "If you were Polish, I'd marry you," even though she was only sixteen and he twenty-three.

"Hi Peter," she said, this time truthfully.

"You said that already!" said Peter, beaming. Still eager, but older and here. Central Park on a Monday afternoon, with a woman he had thought about for eight years, although just now and again, but mostly now, after Susan dumped him for the Taiwanese cellist.

What were the chances, wondered Maitreya, of meeting in Central Park miles from New Jersey and parental disapproval?

"I don't like him," said new best friend Tammy Jo. "If you ask me, he has One Thing on his mind and it's not a Good Thing. For some girls," she added, "he could be nice. But for you, no. I don't think so."

"I'm not looking for anything serious," said Maitreya to Tammy Jo. "Just someone to keep me company on weekends. Or during lunchtime in the city."

"You can find friends under moss, if you lift it high enough," offered Tammy Jo. "Everyone needs a lot of someones. At least twelve people to send Christmas cards to, that's the average. I read it in the paper. Otherwise you're a pathetic loser. I have sixteen, which gives me self-esteem.

"Look at me, MyTree," said Tammy Jo, when no response seemed forthcoming. "Did you think we were going to be friends?"

Maitreya considered the answer. No would be rude. Yes would be wrong.

"Um-num-yup," she said.

"Liar," said Tammy Jo, with satisfaction. "You don't know a thing."

"Tammy Jo?" demanded Peter. "The woman must be eighty and she drinks like a fish."

Fish have no teeth, thought Maitreya. They don't need to floss. The dental article had left an impression only Maitreya understood. Without teeth, no bite. Without bite, no gumption. Without gumption, no go. There was wisdom in tooth maintenance. No joke here. No stalking.

"What do you see in her?" inquired Peter, still waiting for a response. "She's from a farm in South Carolina. She's the only person I've ever heard say 'whupped his ass.' Outside of books, I mean."

"People in the City say it," Maitreya said. "I heard it one day in the office mailroom."

"That's for effect," said Peter. "Office-Broadway. I'm talking about the real thing. Could you really sit down to share a meal with someone who whups ass?"

"I'd holler," said Maitreya dreamily. "I'd run around. But I'd do that. I'd share a meal."

She pushed Peter gently off the Goodwill chair now a shade less blue, chastened with fabric-lightening sunlight all sloshed in through the front windows.

"You go home now," she told him, nudging at him gently.

Peter's internet floral company could keep them both in a downtown apartment, one with silverware and drapes, and it could fund fishing trips as far as Maine. Not yet successful enough for a tiger safari in India, but maybe someday.

Dear Jane, Amanda, Ritu. I am not-quite-in-love with my brother's former tennis partner Peter Nowak who delivers flowers. No, really. Not personally. He runs a company. If you want to say I love you to that special somebody, say it every hour with the power of a flower. Let them know you think of them every minute of the day. Pack a ring into the sixth and final delivery. Will you do me the honor of? Will you be mine? Will you walk in the park, dance in the dark, emulsify fate, serve it with steak? And Po-TAH-toes!

Peter's company could keep them well, and imaginary letters could be written to vanished friends, but Maitreya was satisfied as things were, with her one-bedroom apartment off a highway, a short drive away from the train station in New Jersey.

MEMO NOTES: NEW IDEAS FOR COMPANY EXPANSION

Sixty minutes worth of you / Comes wrapped up in chrysanthy-moo! (in patchwork cow-shaped vase, for an insult/love greeting) REJECTED

We'll live in a house of rosemary and lemon / Just you and me, in our sliver of heaven (in fragrant herbal bouquet, suitable for condiments if romance doesn't pan out) ABSOLUTELY REJECTED

For what my heart so deeply misses / Here are flowers, sixty kisses (in pink vase, bag of Godiva chocolates surrounded by six lilies) ACCEPTED

The love you bring / Makes every hour a fleeting thing / And every note a song to sing (garden medley with plastic bird singing "As Time Goes By" in Frank Sinatra voice when beak toggled down) ACCEPTED, TENTATIVELY

"Whoa!" exclaimed Tammy Jo. "Would that I were creative, but Jack knocked all that out of me. He wanted someone to cook and sew, he couldn't do either, the bastard. Thirty-six years of Velveeta on corn bread, that's what I put up with. If the Good Lord hadn't taken him, I could have used the cleaver on him, all that kicking me around even on the Sabbath. I used to write poetry in high school. My gym teacher, she said I had a chance, even with bad grammar and all, because it's the heart that matters. It's what Oprah always says, and I believe her. We're all poets, she says, deep down we all want the same things."

"Flowers?" said Maitreya doubtfully.

"That too," admitted Tammy Jo, "but mostly love-and-care. What do you think, MyTree?"

"It's true," said Maitreya vaguely, but didn't say the rest. Didn't say, I won't be president of a company, Father. I will not marry a good

Parsi boy, Mother, don't turn so red with fury and self-flagellation. I will not have children who call me Mom and demand food and clothing and video games. I pay my own rent for an apartment and entertain a man who will not marry me nor whom I could love. But it is enough. And I will be happy, at least for now.

"Ohmygoodnessgraciousme, sometimes you are so far away!" said Tammy Jo.

"I'm from India," said Maitreya, blinking. "It's a long way off."

"Are you completely mad?" asked Firoz, who, after Maitreya had just begun her job with Peter's company, received an email photograph of a wrought-metal bird perched drunkenly atop a carafe of poppies with a note reading "Drunk on your love / I rest like a dove" (in considered preference to "I know you'll be hoppy / When I send you these poppies" in a rabbit-shaped cardboard box) with the threat of five more photographed bouquets to follow in immediate succession. "Stop it! I'm your brother and I worry for your well-being. Can't you just write a novel like normal nutheads? Or children's stories about plucky British pubescents like Enid Blyton?"

Maitreya clutched at the telephone wire as if drowning.

"I'm good at this," she said. "The worse I write, the better I get."

"Haven't you heard of aberrations in nature?" said Firoz. "The worst things work beautifully, then collapse all at once for no more reason than they were successful before. The term 'pet rocks' mean anything to you?"

"These are flowers," said Maitreya, a little stiffly, working up her annoyance into a lather, a bowl of egg whites beating up into meringue, a moment more and she could scoop her fury into dollops, drop them on a plate, and fossilize the results. See, this is what becomes of wanting left unattended for too long. Things dry up, one thing becomes another. Sweetness into stone.

"You're riding the mist and just don't know it," said her brother. "One day you'll look down and see nothing beneath your feet, and then— Whoosh! Splash! Splatter!"

"I'm not going to marry Peter, if that's what you mean," said Maitreya. "And he won't marry me."

"Doesn't he think you're sweet?" demanded Firoz.

"Have to go," said Maitreya. "Washing to do. Laundry."

"Of course," said her brother, his voice carrying like filaments of spun glass all the way from Arizona. "How could I forget?"

"Goodbye," said Maitreya, formally, as if she were a court attendant.

"By the way," added Firoz, "you do know Peter followed you around for days before he met you 'accidentally' in the park? I told him where you worked. A stalker with flowers."

"I knew that," lied Maitreya, risen and frothed.

She began to dream soon after, of guns everywhere, hanging from balconies, carried by pigeons, guns with bad teeth looking for dentists, guns that went off in the night all by themselves in empty rooms, guns shooting flowers that turned into blood.

In the mornings she rose swiftly and drove to the train station pretending her dreams were only visiting, old friends in need of her Goodwill armchair to crash on for a night before they left for Montana or India. She did not imagine they could be smoke signals, because even if they were, she would need help with the decoding. In the evenings she drove back from the train station and crept into bed after a frozen chicken dinner, a shower, a changing of the cat's litter box. Nothing was missing from her life. She wished she knew what it wasn't.

On Wednesday evenings, her parents called her from their new split-level on Long Island, their voices tangled with conundrums.

"Priya Malgoankar is coming to visit us tomorrow—with another baby on the way! How difficult it must be for her parents in Mumbai, having to take care of those grandchildren while her husband is busy making millions in Silicon Valley! What a thoughtless girl! And you remember Chotu? He has a job in Palo Alto, doing very well after that Sad Thing. Poor Aradhana—bichara—poor, poor girl, what a tragedy! We will never forget! And that little Anu Menon, big shot professor now, does not keep in touch, even though I sent pedas for Diwali! By UPS! Cost extra fifteen dollars! No manners! What happens to these Indian girls in America, I don't know! And that other fellow, Bansilal from our neighborhood? He has two wives! Two, not one! And perfectly legal, he says, because one of them is married only by Hindu ritual, no papers, so not married at all. And those two lovely children, Rinku and Tinku, one by each wife—so difficult for the grandparents to deal with two different mothers! How on earth do they play all day with those lovely grandchildren with *two* mothers watching? This I cannot say! Chhi! You, beti, are very different. You will reward us one day. Sunnu Auntie always tells me that, she says, Meher, one day your Maitreya will reward you, you wait and see, mark my words. No Evil Eye, choo, kali munther! So, we are happy."

They were a version of Type Two risers, her parents. They woke up speaking and dropped asleep speaking, felled in mid-sentence.

Maitreya shared this observation with Firoz one Saturday, hoping he might ally himself with her for once, sibling solidarity against the omniscience of authority.

"Oh, stop the hullabulla and grow up, Maitreya," sighed Firoz. "Aren't we past insulting our parents? Think of all they've done for us."

He was sighing a lot these days, undone not by the petunia pots but by his dissertation professor, who was now sounding more and more like Don Rickles in a Pinter play, barking out non sequiturs and ominous asides. Firoz was unraveling after ten years at Stanford, his planet ratcheting on the loose, hip-hopping through a universe of red ink and dark motives. The professor had turned conservative after a Baptist revival meeting, and now there was no turning back. *The anti-Americanism of your discussion on world oil standards is beyond logical analysis, descending, I'm afraid, to vituperative nonsense. Might we not substitute reasoned thought for verbal swashbuckling?*

Elizabethan drama, though engaging, is a thing of the past! He was the suit with Pepsi to Firoz's lonely Iran, the televised Republican National Convention to his Moses.

"Really," said Firoz, "why don't you just grow up?"

"She doesn't say y'all," said Maitreya after a pause. "And her hair isn't frosted. It's black with gray streaks, like yours."

"My point is this, MyTree," said Tammy Jo. "You have to have your own point of view. Otherwise, you'll just be barking up the wrong tree, if you get my drift, and who knows what can fall down and knock you out? There's all kinds of fruit up there, and if you'll pardon me, I think your brother is one."

Peter, in his own drift of tide, was out at sea. The flower company was in trouble, not in the usual unsteady way of minor startups but more seriously, with a lawsuit filed in the city offices by an irate narcoleptic divorcé awakened from his nap six times from noon to dusk by a flush of hostas in an evergreen cloud. *With every hosta / My heart beats fosta / Thinking of yew.*

"You idiot!" shouted the divorcé to the six-dollar–an-hour hosta-holder balancing precariously on his bicycle as he handed the flowers over. "This rubbish is from my ex-wife! She's killing me!"

"She paid for it," said the delivery boy indifferently. "Don't kill the messenger."

"I wouldn't bet on that!" replied the bitter divorcé. "You bastard!"

"Heyheyhey!" cried the delivery boy, dodging a blow. "Why don't you just sue somebody?"

"It's not my place to say this, no," observed Tammy Jo, "but he's not to be trusted. Didn't I say so when I met him? He is after One Thing only, and I hope that you have kept it safe. I hope you didn't lose it."

"No, I didn't," said Maitreya. Almost, but didn't. "It's not his fault. The ex-wife should be sued for harassment, not us. If you were forced by your husband to see a film six times in a row, could you sue the movie theater?"

"I don't get it," said Tammy Jo.

Maitreya wasn't sure she knew, either, but it was clear that the lawsuit changed everything, from lunch in the park to company expansion. She had been hoping for a reprieve from copywriting, for an ergonomic chair in a glass-filled room, anticipating exchanging her four mottled thrift-store dresses for black Ann Taylor business suits. She was going to be deep-voiced and wise, pen behind her ear, index finger slanted across her chin, while she ruminated over the white and yellow roses on her desk. Now, let's see—*When you're blue / Roses fill the air in varied hue / And in a snap, the world is color-blasted / —But I just need to sleep, you idiot-bastard!*

Peter was getting married in the spring to Magdalena, a nice girl from Warsaw. *East is West.*

"No problem with the lawsuit," he said to Maitreya. "We have family who'll take care of it."

"Mafia?" asked Maitreya, entirely by accident. *Why can't you just grow up?*

Peter took the question literally. "You sweet thing," he said. "If only you were Polish!"

But Maitreya knew there was more to it. Magdalena's father had a clothing store in Warsaw and London. He was the family who would take care of it, take care of Peter, of Magdalena, of Ann Taylor suits, loving reunions, grandchildren at play, even rejected lovers on the side if they were discreet and kept their peace. He would bless it all under a canopy of stars, a sky clear of pettish planets and tangled wires from Long Island, a vast unfettered stretch of continuity from an old, old country to a new, unfolding one. She was not part of any of this, not in a million years, how could she be, with her blue Goodwill chair in a third-floor apartment overlooking a dusty street? Like Ritu, she had gone home, she had completely vanished and was only remembered in postcards carried to and fro, without the right address, across the seas.

"I'm so happy for you," she said to Peter, and they were both relieved that she meant it.

There was no phone call from Firoz that Saturday morning, which was not at all surprising, given the way fate had carried them both, sister and brother, to the brink and back, like a camel confused by high-rises in the desert.

I will carry you someday, Maitreya promised chance, promised her parents, clinking a metal teaspoon against her china cup. She rebelled against laundry, preferring the complexities of last Sunday's crossword puzzle to fill her morning: 6 Across, 4 Down, *and a hootenanny swirl.* She was dancing in space, clear of Dear Abby and earthquakes, no longer put upon to make sense of the world, delighting in her orphaned joy. With her pencil she drew on the newspaper the barrel of a gun pointing skyward and a bullet flying up, flying free. But the more she gazed at her doodle, the more it became a tunnel in the ground, the bullet a rabbit falling inward, deep into a hole, and she followed it with a circling finger, spiraling in bright darkness, for who knew what tomorrow would bring.

Tintinnabulations

SIDDHARTH VELLODI STOOD at the open window looking over a city street so calm and gray it could have been a river. Buildings rose like banks on every side, slanted alleyways ran narrow and quiet between them, tributaries without sound or ripple. From his vantage point up on the fourth floor of the office complex, the view beneath seemed less of a place than of a painting, an illusion given its lie only by a sudden motorcar that appeared from a bend and disappeared behind another, an interruption without meaning, without cause or consequence. Then the street was quiet again, as if nothing had happened at all, a stillness without history. He breathed in the air, relishing his moment of privacy. Soon he'd walk down the back stairway of the building and out into the asphalt parking lot three short blocks to the east. There he'd slide into his metal gray Toyota, turn on the ignition, and return home to a life of maneuvered traffic, of decisions and forced banter. This was the way every evening now came to a close, after the offices had emptied and the noise and rush subsided.

He crossed over to his desk. A maze of papers lay scattered there, waiting to be sorted through, discarded, gathered. Some things would have to be said, some left unfinished. This was his last day in this office, though no one knew, not even Nina. The divorce papers would have to be signed in time to come, but first the subject broached.

Inserted into dialogue, the right tone caught and held, a pact agreed upon and sealed past the guard lines of tight-throated pleasantries. The shaming art of cleaving. The child must be told, explained to. Somewhere in the days ahead, an airplane ticket bought, a job approached as fresh and all-consuming. Each position he'd held— professor, businessman, and now Silicon Valley entrepreneur—each came with its own unsteady promises and mocking sureties.

One hundred thousand dollars, even more, up in the air. After the chemotherapy, the bills, the money left uncounted and unaccounted for in those muddled months.

Got your knickers in a twist, did it? inquired Nina once the disease had been beaten down and left to founder meekly in her tart rejoinders. The Big C. She was nothing of the girl he had married years ago, the quiet bride gazing down at her hands, the diffident bookish woman tongue-tied before his faculty colleagues, the intense young mother with her laughing child. In South Bend the years had come together in a jumble, and her illness had revealed their blackened core. Unsettled by her fury, he'd kept his distance. What a cliché, he thought, to be gutted into silence by illness and dwindling bank accounts.

You can leave, she'd said boldly one afternoon after another flailing spat, not thinking he would. For me, there's always tomorrow.

And tomorrow and tomorrow. Siddharth remembered how that flare-up ended. Lighting fools another way. A phrase to mock them later as they scoured blindly through empty cardboard boxes in a bus depot when hope had quieted, like actors lingering on a stage after the final curtain call.

Siddharth sifted through the papers, a slow deliberation of choices and rejections. So much to be rid of, some to retain. He picked up the signed job offer to be mailed by noon tomorrow. He paused at the divorce documents and read briefly again through the heavy legalese, as if the pause itself were an apology, a way of reconsidering the past. He saw the sentimentality of this gesture, the worthlessness of conscience for a mind already steeled against injunctions. But what would he tell the child?

Out of habit, he dusted the empty office table with the flat of his hand, a movement carried over from his days as a faculty member in Ithaca, when student papers inked in with mathematical stutters and inconsistencies littered his office desk. Red ink, frustration, lost tenure. Neither researcher nor teacher. A tolerable father, an indifferent spouse. His hand swept over the desk, a quick movement across offenses great and small. The desktop remained gritty, his efforts leaving a clear path like a city street, a tributary without purpose. Everywhere the stubborn dust a rejoinder to a stumbling hope. He walked down the stairway, balancing a briefcase against his chest, a suitcase in his hand. As he entered the stairwell, he heard the telephone on his desk begin to ring. Three days in a row, the telephone rang precisely at this time. Twice he'd answered: no one there. A clown, a fool, a broken line. By intention or accident, he couldn't tell.

Once, a voicemail: I knew before you did. She told me first.

Some loon, some teenage kid without the pressures of an evening's homework.

The sky had darkened; night fell suddenly this time of year, tripping shadows into stars and moonlight. Siddharth unlocked the car door, slid his bags into a corner of the car, and turned on the radio. Out of habit, he checked his watch: 6:35. He leaned back into his seat, breathing deeply, drawing in the picture of the calm gray street, willing it into his mind for a place of rest. Voices rose on NPR, discussing terrorism: motives, methods, outcomes, speculations faltering into digressions. McVeigh was fervently resurrected, human psychology debated, universal motives linked to 9/11, Afghanistan, Iraq. The voices chorused into a medley, planing into one another, upending all the years. Siddharth flipped the switch to another channel. Sounds of Mozart filled the car.

The telephone had stopped ringing in his office room long before he'd even reached the parking lot.

Maitreya couldn't for the life of her write another poem.

"Well, those weren't really poems," said her husband Mohan kindly. "They're just rhyming words. 'Every hour. Flower shower.' Ad copy."

He was in the oil business, in a career rife with deals and negotiations, and with ample cash to spare, he looked generously upon his childless wife. He hoped they'd have a host of children, a football league, a cricket team, or at least a boy, at least one, maybe, with a shock of black hair and a sharp impertinence.

"A television child," said Maitreya, but her husband had no idea what she meant.

She took to dreaming in the early days of their marriage of a little girl in pigtails, but this girl in dreams was as tall as a house and answered to Lemon Heaven.

Her husband found the nomenclature puzzling.

"That sounds like a light souffle," he said to Maitreya, encouraging her culinary talents, which till now were robustly nonexistent.

Sometimes Maitreya woke up in the middle of the night and said out loud, and quite clearly, "Stop the hullabulla!" or "Ohgoodnessgraciousme! Enid Blyton is my tennis partner."

Her husband, ever solicitous, offered back rubs and hot sweet tea as solace, which was a gesture quite redundant, because Maitreya refused to acknowledge any lapses in her character or larynx.

"I *never* said that," she'd say firmly, and that was that.

At times she'd wander in her sleep, peripatetic and blowsy in long white nightgowns like some Brontë heroine fettered in a sweltering Mumbai flat, swatting away imaginary mosquitoes and mumbling indecipherable rhymes.

One evening, just before Nina telephoned from America to say to her mother that Siddharth was off to California and not returning to South Bend, not now, not ever, Maitreya remembered she'd once been the sole possessor of a fuzzy blue armchair.

"Funny thing is," said Maitreya, "I'd quite forgotten its existence."

She dreamed that night of the chair in a third-floor apartment overlooking a street full of meandering buffaloes and angry, honking delivery trucks. She could swear she heard a child weaving through the traffic, some small impatient thing calling out for toffee, and the deeper she sank into her chair, the further went the child into a forest full of broken bones and diamonds. Overhead an airplane flew, trailing sequined gowns and trains of bloodied velvet.

I had a dream, she said to her husband, shaking him vigorously as he groaned beside her, half asleep at two a.m. He had an early morning meeting with an Arab sheik and a Belgian CEO; a salary spike lay in the offing if he made a good impression. But he had to have a full night's sleep to be alert and charming before breakfast.

"Good, good," he said, encouraging and sympathetic, and turned over on his side.

How gently he snored, like a peaceful dragon ranging the forests in pajamas, his chest rising and falling in syncopated rhythm, mild domesticated beast of the sleeping wilds.

Hosha stood frowning over an open suitcase in a London flat while his mother wondered out loud if he would ever return. I will, he'd said, to soothe her anxious fluttering, knowing he would not. He would lose all points of return, even to himself. Some winter mornings, in another city in another country, he'd rise groggily to brush his teeth and find reflected in the cracked bathroom mirror the split image of a familiar and passing stranger. A broken vase, a bleeding finger, a thing to be restored. Hello, he'd think, steadying himself against the cold washbasin. My name is Hosha, my provenance a sneeze.

Chotu Sharma, on the day Siddharth left for California, mentioned to his wife that he was a California Guy (as he'd put it earlier to his relatives back in India). His wife was unimpressed, familiar by now with Chotu's flailing attempts at verbal assimilation—but his relatives were astonished and admiring, imagining Sharma alternately as a movie star or a Silicon Valley salesman-king, minions clustered at his feet holding laptops aloft in supplication. Sharma permitted such illusions;

they didn't contest his ambitions. His checklist was complete: a coiffed American wife, a blue Mustang, a gabled brick house. Vacations in Hawaii and a portfolio with stocks that rose every morning like the sun. Not for him the anxiety of influence, but rather its full-throated celebration.

He hardly ever thought about his childhood. If you mentioned the Menon girls, he made an elaborate pretense of remembering, but claimed not to have known them. He preferred to keep memories of taunts and terrors to a minimum in his life. He had washed away his sins in Coca-Cola and bonhomie; everyone agreed he was a splendid fellow.

He would never meet Siddharth, even though they would come to live within a few hundred miles of each other in Southern California. He had no need to revisit the past, though he remained wary of imperious mothers. Sharma was an invention, patented and appropriated by his own uncertain yearning. He was, he said with pride, an American.

Most people, it must be acknowledged, would be pleased to have a red Ferrari in their garage. At first Sally Johnstone (wife of Timothy Johnstone and part-time artist and full-time mother of Maddie and Winnie in Dearborn, Michigan) was confused, mistaking her neighbor's ebullience as an announcement of his wife's welcome first pregnancy. Her neighbor had a tendency to speak in metaphors drawn from sources of acquisition and barter, an extension of his excellent business acumen. Janet has a Ferrari in the garage! Finally!

Congratulations! she said enthusiastically, but still a little doubtful. (A bun in the oven?)

Got it from the dealership, said her neighbor James Hanrahan the Second.

He preferred to write his name without the common Roman numerals; extended spelling gave his name a courtly sweep and his midwestern lineage a kind of royalty, like Henry the Fourth or Charles the First. And he had been to England, where the Queen was still addressed on the BBC or the street with respectful distance or rude irony, both variants, he believed, of hurt exclusion. James Hanrahan wished to be included, even if only in his own business-focused mind.

Been in an accident, so it was cheap. For a Ferrari, he added, making clear that a beat-up Ferrari was still a Ferrari.

Ah, congratulations! said Sally again, marshaling enthusiasm in a fresh direction.

You said that already! said a beaming James Hanrahan. Check it out! You and Tim—come over, why don't you? We'll take you for a spin. This weekend?

Sure, said Sally, given to good fellowship and consensus after three decades of Sunday Bible Study in church basements. We'll be there Saturday morning. If that's okay? She was never sure if James was entirely serious in his invitations or merely advertising his possessions. His pronouncements seemed posed and stilted, like the way he set up mannequins in department store windows in Chicago for his line of creaseless dress shirts.

James Hanrahan (the Second, father of a Third in fourteen months, though he was not to know this yet) rose a little higher in his gleaming handmade Oxfords. You guys come right over Saturday morning, he said.

Sally Johnstone and James H. the Second returned to their separate houses, no more to say for the moment.

The Ferrari was indeed red and parked in the garage, as still as cold butter in a dish. Years ago it had been less stationary, driven frequently and wildly through green fields and city streets in Minnesota before a last and fatal crash. Now it had been reconstituted by Italian mechanics and made new and whole, though something of its provenance remained in the chassis, causing James Hanrahan to brake and look over his shoulder sharply one September afternoon while he was driving to Chicago, as if he sensed a presence there.

In the very moment Sally Johnstone went into her house that Friday evening and shut the door, Siddharth Vellodi stepped into his own gray Toyota in an empty parking lot a few hundred miles away in South Bend, bags in hand. He would never know of that red Ferrari, or even care. No Hanrahan or Johnstone would ever cross his troubled path. A stranger's life stirs up the dust, then spools away without a trace into landscapes and weathers past envisioning. Every story navigates its own occluded road.

Chinoy himself was not around to witness any part of these brief convergences and eddies, carried lightly into history, now insubstantial as air.

Hi Nilufer/Maitreya, wrote Talina, tentatively, on a picture postcard of a jolly, laughing man in a capacious cheddar-cheese hat. *I hope life's being good to you in steamy Mumbai!* Sometimes spring in rural Wisconsin was as cold and distancing as winter, the eaves frozen, the horizon a thin blue line. Huddled cattle moving through the snow-lit nights like drifting umbra. *Just thought to say hello after all these years. Mum said I should write. It's been so long....* The words lay numb and stupid, stilled in their bleak yearning. Then she tore the card up into a mess of little pieces, leaving only a scrap with the man's open, grinning mouth like an abandoned Cheshire Cat.

At 6:35 in the evening, just before the shadows darkened into night one early March, Nina was clearing out her cavernous kitchen cupboard, six deep and rowdy rows of shelving stuffed with items of all bulk and shape jostling and sliding over one other. Yesterday she'd attacked the bedroom dresser with the same intense attention—out went a decade of old socks and ragged nightgowns and frayed underthings. Nesting, her yoga instructor at the Y had once murmured soothingly to her; she had heard the word before, some memory connected to a book club. It's what women do when preparing to give birth or after terrible trauma, like an illness. A thoughtful man, he did not say it out aloud: *cancer.* A primitive urge, he explained, to tamp down the sod before the harvest, or just after, a winnowing of the soul. Nina felt an uncharitable urge to winnow her instructor but understood his kindness even if it bounced off her like a thudding bowling ball.

Things had gathered on the kitchen shelves over the years, like sediment, layer upon unwieldy layer of broken pencils, bottle tops, cookbooks, can openers, silver spoons, a mini-colander, three twisted skewers, a bundle of old tax forms, a jam jar full of shells, a penknife, a pink piggy bank, empty biscuit tins, a skein of ribbon.

Out they went, right into the garbage bin, a toss, a toss, a toss. The knife with the broken handle gave Nina pause, something almost remembered—or was it a leftover from Maya's last art project? She puzzled over the penknife for just a moment before it went into the rising pile of rubbish.

Soon Maya would be home after her clarinet lesson at the conservatory. Soon Siddharth would walk in, briefcase in hand, anticipating a restful evening, a hot dinner.

Soon the night shadows would deepen, turn to black.

As the telephone rang and rang in an empty South Bend office, Anu blew gently on a dandelion weightless in the palm of her hand, scattering its seeds across the faint spring grass in a southern university quadrangle.

That's the fluffiest dandelion ever, her lover Jeannette marveled.

She loves me, she loves me not.

I think she loves me.

If you followed those wisps, you'd never know. How they dissipated into the evening.

In two weeks, it would be Maya's eleventh birthday. What do you send an eleven-year-old girl? No birthday present seemed quite right.

You think too much, said Jeannette. Give her a book. Or chocolates. She'll just be glad you remembered her.

She blew lightly into her hands and leaned into Anu's shoulder.

It's cold, she said. And windy. Early for dandelions.

Simulacra

SAN DIEGO IS a vexing tooth. The kind you can't pull out or just leave there, a filament of pain under the gums demanding both dismissal and attention. A threat, minor but insistent. A looming gap. An anchored presence. A nuisance. Still, Nina is unfazed by this, her first journey anywhere in years. And no wonder. She has withstood another kind of menace—a cancer survivor, she is called by her neighbors in South Bend, the sort of term you wear awkwardly like a borrowed hat, an ill-fitting defense against other losses too untenable to name. Outwardly she is the same as always, a slight woman with a sharply angled face and a lithe but softening frame, something between a ferret and a kitten. Her gray pencil skirt and black leather handbag lend her a severity she assumes when meeting strangers, as she must in a few minutes—her ex-husband Siddharth and his wife, their old familiarity just a memory, and this new encounter a cautious negotiation.

Nina steps out onto the tarmac, into the hot San Diego sun, suddenly caught in a wash of unmitigated light. Blinded for a moment, she catches her breath to steady her after five hours in the plane's cool and dimly droning interior. Sunlight blazes everywhere, stripping her of reference and history; she is breathlessly incandescent, looking for relief from the glare.

"Ooh, it's hot!" announces the child beside her, shaking out her long brown hair as she slips her hand into Nina's. But she is just a child, and so for her, heat, like broccoli or nightly prayers, is just a fact of life not to be contested. The child is not complaining.

"We'll walk to that big building there," says Nina, pretending confidence and pointing to the terminal a hundred feet away. "They'll be waiting."

The child picks up her pace, skips and hops a little in anticipation. She wears a purple cotton skirt with bright silver sequins, and on her hair is a pink velvet Alice band. Her tiny beaded black purse jangles against her hips as she moves, creating a stir, a hint of music, reminding Nina of the silver anklets she wore as a child. The child dips her head left to right, right to left, in pace with each skip she takes. She is like a monkey or a princess. A monkey princess.

"I feel happy," says the child. Now she's skipping like a feather buffeted in the wind.

"If I hold my breath," wonders the child, "can I stop time and always be happy? If I count to ten or a hundred?"

The child is full of questions.

"You can't do that," says Nina reasonably. "Then you'd be a ghost. Only ghosts stop time."

"I can be a ghost," says the child, delighted. "Boo!"

The child is incorrigible.

Nina is a little out of breath with pulling along two heavy carry-ons, one of which holds an expensive present. A Kanjeevaram russet sari with a gold brocade border for the new wife, who (it was explained to her over the telephone by Siddharth) likes all things Indian. The new wife is an excellent sous-chef as well as a top real estate agent. This stellar combination fails to unnerve Nina, a woman with the fortitude of one who has long battled unsympathetic realtors and her Homeowners Association, both disapproving of her disorderly management skills, her once-white picket fence and overgrown front lawn. Now with two mortgage payments past due and under threat of foreclosure, Nina has resorted to domestic rituals for sustenance. She steams bland mountains of basmati rice to assuage her anxiety. She scouts the Food Network for recipes introduced with the magical phrase *Scale of Difficulty: EASY*. It's astonishing how many recipes fall into this category—and not just rice and pasta but tandoori chicken, chocolate cake, rasam. The results, as the child tripping along beside her often protests, range from laudable to regrettable (or in the child's more robust opinion, either *mmm, okay,* or *eeew!*). For Nina, convenience trumps quality. Siddharth, on the other hand, never shied away from effort, scouting always for the better thing, the better make (*Scale of Difficulty: CHALLENGING*), though his ambitions in the early days were humbler, limited to hunting down gourmet coffee packets in grocery aisles with the single-mindedness of a colonial explorer.

Nina has admitted to herself that the new wife is the most gourmet of coffee packets, a superior version of Nina's former self—younger, smarter, rich in empathy, all of which Nina lacks, especially now when being on her own has turned her into a bristle-brush with feet—or so she thinks. She takes offense quickly and mines everyday parlance for offhand betrayals or camouflaged insults. But she remains brisk and focused. The secret is not to become a wet rag, a mop, a bore. This is what I've come to, she thinks. A life measured by a catalogue of domestic touchstones, an imagination powered by the very condition it resists.

Nina and the child have packed their belongings in just two pieces of hand luggage because they don't plan to stay long in San Diego, just five days. Nina's excuse, prim as befits an adjunct professor of English, is that work beckons—doesn't it always?—though if truth be told, Nina has no summer job; her teaching contract resumes in September. So the carry-ons contain a mismatched clutch of underthings and shirts (the extra in case of mishaps or spills, for no matter if one is four or forty-something, accidents are possible, anything can happen, anywhere, at any time; this is a lesson to be learned). Jeans, a swimsuit, T-shirts, dresses, and a salwar kameez. The requisite toothbrush and cosmetics. Their luggage is tightly packed. The brocade-border sari will need to be ironed before presentation, and Nina can only hope the expensive chocolates for Siddharth have not melted. He was a fool for sweet things. Is a fool for this new one who cooks and sells houses like lemonade.

The child is at an age where everything is a wonder—a snail, a phrase, marbled cookies. No terrain for her is awkward, neither tarmac nor open sky from which she has just descended like a chirpy god. Nina, earthbound with prudence, can only marvel; the ground beneath her feet is hard and gritty, ready to give way in a clatter of pebbles or careening fear. But the child, half airborne, seems to fly.

"Look, Mom!" the child sings, as if on cue, hopping and skipping, arms extended like an airplane, her black bag twirling. Nina is forced to hurry gracelessly beside this dervish, suggesting to fellow passengers tramping onward at either side of them that a family or eager lover awaits her at the gate.

"Look at my feet!" The child is tap-dancing, hip-hopping, any moment now she will trip and land on her nose, and what kind of entrance to San Diego will that be? Bloodied, Nina expected that, but not literally.

"That's lovely," says Nina. "But stop now. We're almost there."

There is no one at the gate.

"They'll be waiting inside the terminal," says Nina anxiously. Or perhaps they won't. Perhaps they've gone home.

Her apprehension lifts and falls in hiccups. She remembers why her neighbor Alice was suspicious of so wayward a journey. You're going to visit your *ex*? And he's *married*? A situation that deleted two possibilities at once. Not a potential husband. Not even a recoverable one. But other friends were sympathetic. Closure, said one, as if Siddharth were a zipper left undone.

She sees the two of them now by the big glass front doors and is momentarily surprised that they look so small against the towering panes, even if such a distortion is only an illusion of geometry and distance. Siddharth had once seemed larger than life; perhaps that was the illusion. A man always in flight, even their conversations held in transit as he entered or left the house, the car, the marriage. A marriage needn't fail; it can just pass you by. Now he seems slight and immobile, has lost twenty pounds, peering lightly through his horn-rimmed glasses at her, his black hair thinning at the temples. He is dressed in brown corduroy pants and a white open-necked shirt. His nose is still a quick straight line, not sensuous, almost paternal, his lips thin blades, although his skin has absorbed a sallow sheen from the California sun. He is elegant in a cufflinks-and-striped-tie sort of way. Nina takes inventory of this strange familiar man, testing his new substance against memory, seeing how all the parts and hinges fall into place like a door firmly shut. The child hides shyly behind Nina.

So many hugs! And welcomes. And this new wife, her name is Laurie, a pliable friendly word denoting hope and brightness. She is taller than Siddharth by half a head, her face is high cheekboned and sculpted, the nose slightly askew as if challenging the pretensions of the face. Her light green sundress falls in a precipice over her flat stomach. She exercises daily, runs a mile, eats organic. Nina breathes in quickly, must stop herself immediately. Enough of this. She must extend her arms. She must unbristle and flow. She hugs Laurie.

"Welcome," says Laurie cheerfully, and Nina is disconcerted by so heartfelt a reception.

The child peeps out from behind Nina, unprepared for this commotion. Welcome, cry these sudden hosts, to her, to the world it seems. Welcome, welcome!

No one thinks to stop speaking in the SUV as it hurtles homeward. Siddharth is full of questions and observations, careful with his phrasing, shaping words deliberately. He speaks little of himself, though, saying nothing of the move from Los Angeles last year, the burgeoning software company, the possibility of a partnership with his Korean boss. Seven years is a breath in suspended time.

News of Siddharth's rising career has come to Nina via gossipy relatives in India, second-, third-, fourth-hand, in a looping arc of connections like a train with too many stops. But now he chatters on, the old breezy airiness to his words lifting her half-dazed into a pleasant stupor. You'd think he was a brother, all this family talk with no reference to their shared and jumbled past. How are her parents back home—in Bangalore now, are they? The north too cold for them? He's sorry to know her father's almost blind, difficult for a man who loved reading the newspaper every morning. A shame! And Maitreya, the woman in Jersey—the oil magnate's wife? Did you get the wedding invitation? (He has a name, thinks Nina, mildly irritated. Mohan, not OilMagnate.) And he's heard little Anu in Alabama won't marry Steven, that poor sod, after all these years. Well, not that little, she must be—what? at least forty? forty-five? Time goes by! Why not marry Steven? He could someday be vice president at Intel, even move to India if she wanted! Wouldn't that make her parents happy? Anu needs a man! And Jeannette, thinks Nina, is his name. He's a she and wears suspenders. They'd marry if it were legal in Alabama. This information she doesn't share; why qualify the moment? Siddharth's voice floats over them, miasmic but still insistent in its grilling. And that Talina-Malina-Something girl, the one who sent us Christmas cards? Who does that these days? Who has the time? Heard she's still in Wisconsin with some loser. And you? The teaching job going well? Mostly boring stuff, or are you on to poetry and Shakespeare, things of that sort? I remember one—My love is like a red, red rose . . . oh wait, that's Burns! And to think I memorized Shakespeare's sonnets in high school! Apparently I can no longer summon up a remembrance of things past! And what about Indian writers these days—they're all over the place, lift a page and you'll find one holding forth! Did you notice they're getting younger every day? O Rushdie, where art thou? And your health! (He won't mention cancer. Past history. Why sully this jolly day?) What about your allergies? And peanuts—I remember how badly you reacted to our visit to the peanut farm in Valparaiso! Your skin in hives! And that peanut butter scare last spring—in Florida, was it, or Texas?—so much for the overhauled FDA! The more things change!

A silence ensues for a moment, but Nina can see hanging in the air !!! and yet more !!!! The car is full of unspoken !!!!! She stifles a laugh, turns it into a cough. So many exclamation points, all lined up in a row—not bowling pins, not things to strike, just muddled armature she must not cross.

Nina is contrite. Her presence has brought on this welter of verbiage from Siddharth in which she will drown if she pays the slightest attention. And she feels a guilt she can barely repress. His violent patter, this artillery of good cheer that arises out of helplessness—he will pummel her with it in rounds through the coming days until she puts a stop to it, until she shuts him up, it's her hand now on the latch. But she will wait out the line of fire, and she will forgive without the burden of acknowledgment or confession.

So Nina turns to Laurie and tells her how much she has been looking forward to this visit. Laurie, taken unawares, says this is why she loves India, people are so open and without guises. She means this new incarnation of Siddharth, of course, some new saintlike entity with whom Nina has not yet been acquainted.

But still, in this way they have each cleaned out a window. The child is hiding in a seat at the back of the SUV, humming something incomprehensible and muted.

The house is as she expected it to be, a tidy white structure with three square bedrooms, a pebbled driveway, and a shingled roof like the one over her own childhood home in Dehradun. A home she'd left behind for good, despite her mother's ambivalence, for marriage, and then for a life of paperwork and lecture halls in towns across monochromatic midwestern states.

Nina looks confidently at this child beside her; this one will not leave home—never, not once, not even for school. She's right here where she wants her. Nina wants to laugh, but the sound is impossible, twisted in her throat.

At the end of so many missing worlds, this seamless house.

"Let me give you the Grand Tour," says Laurie, not in the least ironic.

Nina remembers that Laurie is a real estate whiz.

The living room, sedate in teak furniture and swaths of burgundy and cream, abuts a dining room with hardwood floors and a kitchen with shining stainless-steel appliances. The bedrooms, flush off a narrow hallway, are subdued in shades of beige. The whole place drips with Victorian chandeliers hung like giant earrings from every ceiling. These fixtures seem at odds with the stucco siding, a house uncertain of its provenance—and thereby an apt fit for Siddharth. Neither Indian nor American, an eclectic man rather than a man with eclectic tastes. Nina wonders if his friends call him Sid.

"You won't believe the deal we got on this casa," says Laurie, all proud energy and focus. "Thanks to the economy."

Still not a shade of irony. No hint of *their misfortune is my joy*. Nina envies such directness. She opens her mouth to say something supportive and cheerleading but thinks instead of foreclosures and sheriff's sales. But Indiana is far away, at least for now.

Most exciting is the pool in the backyard, shaped like a giant kidney bean.

How beautiful it is, like the sea. The house is ten miles away from the Pacific Ocean, deep inland, so this curve of water substitutes well. The pool is an eye-opener for the child, who is not used to such extravagance in South Bend. She squeals in joy and skitters sideways like a pony before an undulating field of blue. Where she comes from, the winters are long and gusty-noisy, snow angels and hot chocolate soothing the small ravages of chilled toes and dripping noses. In California, every day is a balm with nothing resistant to pit life against. This is why, Nina tells herself again, she is here: to rest in golden suspension, to drift in amber.

"It's been too long," observes Laurie brightly, offering Nina a glass of lemonade as she sits by the pool trailing lines with her feet in the silken water. "You must come often. This is your home too. Isn't it, Marvin?"

A fat black cat curled under her chair glares suspiciously at Nina. *As if.*

"Thank you. Yes, of course," says Nina dutifully, though she wonders where this gathering will eventually lead, into what unstated complicity or guttered pause.

Laurie is kind, like a mother, except that Nina does not need one, must instead be one. She loves the sari, admires the intricate brocade border.

"Can you imagine anyone working on this *by hand*?" she says, her index finger tracing the waves and whorls of filigree on the shimmering cloth. "This must have taken *weeks*!"

The cat yawns, unimpressed.

"Marvin loves it," says Laurie. "Don't you, Marvin?"

Laurie will wear the sari in a day or two, after she's ironed out the creases. Nina promises to help drape it around her, each pleat descending in a courtly sweep. Laurie will be an Indian princess. Siddharth has gallantly pronounced the chocolates his favorite brand.

All is well. Tomorrow they will visit SeaWorld, and then the zoo with its huffing, chuffing train.

Still, Nina is attentive only in part. She is intent on watching the child jump in and out of the water with a giant rubber ducky-dinghy around her waist. Next year the child will have to take swimming classes. This summer Nina must watch over her, call out cautionary directives:

"Not so deep!"

"Get back here!"

"Move to the left!"

Siddharth and Laurie look briefly at each other. Laurie raises an eyebrow. She seems worried, perhaps because she has no children. A displacement of sympathy, thinks Nina, for which there really is no need. Nina feels an unexpected rush of affection, a stab of happiness. It catches her unawares, like a birthing cramp.

A walk around the neighborhood, then, to shake off the pool water, to breathe in the California afternoon. So salubrious it is, so energizing, Nina can almost feel each breath she takes fill her body with a lightness she can scarcely bear. "I'm like a balloon," she whispers to the child, who is tugging at her fingers, pulling her along. She seems to float behind the child, such a wafting celebration. She could be a burst of colors all on her own. The moment passes. Stray clouds lengthen across the afternoon sky, joy stretched into vapor.

"Hungry," announces the child. She's getting a little withered by the brilliant camaraderie of this day.

"Me too," says Nina, surprising herself, embarrassed to be heard aloud.

Siddharth and Laurie have caught only the second part of this exchange. *Me too.* They walk step in step like a set of casual soldiers. They too. They two. Onward and upward, thinks Nina, here I am. Here we go. A small unpracticed army, they cross a row of crooked streets with houses pushing eagerly toward the curb, windows, doors, all clustered and spilling into inadequate little front yards. Yards poised as if in motion, waiting for a starting gun to sound their clumsy charge. A tricycle upended, a row of empty terracotta flowerpots, a garden hose left unattended on a driveway, inexplicable white drifts of a toilet roll hanging from a window.

Metal, mud, mortar, concrete, paper.

Nina touches her wrist briefly. Blood and stone.

An ice cream truck jingles out into the street, as if sent on cue. Who's for ice cream?

Everyone, it seems. Vanilla all around. Vanilla people. Just everyday sorts with a yen for candy sprinkles, candy bits, gummies, nuts. Nina and the child opt for sprinkles. Siddharth smiles vaguely, as if such excesses are far beyond his ken. His ice cream cone is left plain, without adornment. A solid swirl without nuance on a sugar cone.

Laurie will have gummies.

"Yummy gummies," Laurie says aloud, and brightly, as if to amuse the child. Who is not amused, or even listening. Instead the child is naming the colors on her sprinkles, picking each one out with a trampoline-jumpy finger. Orange, blue, green, yellow, white, purple, black, pink, violet, red. And because of the punishing humidity of the afternoon heat, a runny one in violet-red. The child counts these colors quickly. Ten-almost-eleven.

On the way home, they are accosted by a man with a very large black mustache, the razor-thin edges of which look primed for battle.

The rain in Spain stays mainly on the plain, says the man politely, with just a hint of menace. He must be about sixty years old, guesses Nina. The rest of him seems an unlikely battlefield. His hair is not more than a profusion of erratic silver lines across a shining pate. His trousers are a worn brown corduroy, and his white shirt shows ancient signs of mustard and ketchup, even a streak of black grease, its origins uncertain. The man is German or pretending to be. He ends his sentences with "*nein*"—confusing Nina, who imagines this an abbreviated sobriquet to address her in some familiar if occluded manner.

The rain in Spain stays mainly on the plain, *nein*?

On the contrary, says Nina a bit stiffly, my belief is that it rains everywhere in Spain, though possibly with greater velocity and frequency on the plain, if you say so.

The could-be-German man eyes her unsympathetically.

There are wars, he says. In Palestine, Israel, Syria, the Congo, Ukraine. Airplanes are blown up, people are kidnapped. Areas around the South China Sea are not promising tourist destinations. The prognosis for the world is just not good, any way you cut it. All these things are possible or already here. Your ice cream is vanilla. Your ex-husband prefers it plain. Sprinkles are a lie, unless they're in Spain and of the hydraulic variety. The weather everywhere is in your head.

Stop, commands the child, tugging at Nina's fingers. *Stopstopstop!*

A dream is like an ice cream cone, gratifying but impermanent.

Dreams stop time, objects the could-be-German, looking injured.
Boo!

Here we are, cries Laurie. They have reached the tidy house with its dripping, lighted chandeliers. Home again!

By evening, the child is asleep suddenly without warning (but not unexpectedly, after all that swimming and busy skittering), collapsing into a deep and intense silence. Nina tucks a cotton sheet around the child's slumbering body, lifting her wet tresses away from her face, combing them outward, soft spokes radiating from a sun. Her fingers rake the pillow. "Sleep, baby," whispers Nina to a child who cannot hear her.

This is Laurie's story:

Laurie is an only child, Californian to the core. When she was three, her parents moved to Scotland, close to Inverness, where her mother comes from. Her father, a man who made his small fortune in agribusiness, grapes and corn mostly, found Scotland hospitable but the terrain stubbornly resistant to American fertilizers. Her mother never wanted to return, but return they did, and Laurie went to school in Sacramento, then to college in Los Angeles, where she worked at a rental agency until this move to San Diego. One day she hopes to open a restaurant, not fancy but elegant and simple, the healthful basics with flair—wholegrain watercress sandwiches, lemon-infused granola cupcakes, soy yogurt shakes. Her improbable specialty is makki ki roti with coq au vin. Dhaba cuisine meets Chez Panisse.

"That doesn't *sound* good," admits Laurie. "But really, it's delicious."

Nina pulls lettuce leaves apart in a capacious salad bowl. Perhaps a leaf could pick up traction, become a magic wand. She could wave it and turn them all into chicken liver. Lunch for Marvin.

"Perhaps an upscale café by the beach, if we can swing the required capital," Laurie says. "That would be nice."

Laurie has left Siddharth out of the story, saving him for another day. Or perhaps out of diplomacy or politeness. Nina would like to know more but is careful not to ask. Each to her own unfolding. How simple, thinks Nina, the sheer precision of such details to describe a life. Nothing messy when you chart and tabulate the facts. Here is where I started; here I am now. A ladder on which each rung is hammered soundly, not a slip or creaky slat.

She does not feel any better acquainted with Laurie, though.

The details are not luminous. They guard Laurie lightly, opaque and hard.

At night the adults sit around the oval kitchen table under a watchful antique wrought iron clock that chimes the hour. The television blares a range of noises, full-throated to muted susurrations. An update on a plane lost last week over a war-torn area. A whodunit in process, human or technological failure? Microphones are held up to demand witness. *What did you see? How do you feel?* Curious faces crowd the screen—aged villagers, eager reporters, even a wide-eyed boy walking a Pekingese. Flashes of objects found. A Minnie Mouse pencil box, the painted cartoon on the lid still intact after the living are gone. A flapping shirtsleeve, a singed brown suitcase, a woman's gold-toned black handbag. Wolf Blitzer worries tirelessly in tones to match this visual orchestra. In the background flash a tumbling rush of images: air crashes of yore, a pin-stripe-suited expert on aviation, a yellow chart with assorted flight data, a general in blue uniform pontificating on the trials of aerial combat, puffs of gray smoke and falling black debris. Such spinning shards of color, a frantic Guernica.

The three of them sit quietly at the table. The first shadows are gathering in the room; the dusk becomes a tender presence. The television is switched off, the world recedes, and now the kitchen is awash with friendly sounds—a blender whirs, a pot bubbles, a singing wisp of steam escapes a kettle. Anyone looking in might think they were a family.

Dinner is wheat bread, salad, a coriander fish stew, and apple tart. The food is delicious; Laurie *is* a good cook. All the ingredients, as Nina has suspected, are organic. She cannot eat the salad in its nest of bitter nettles, but Laurie has no such queasy hesitation (and neither does Siddharth, who once dismissed all greens as cattle fodder). The crystal wine decanter is open, tall stemmed glasses stand stiffly by their china dinner plates. Decanters, not bottles, thinks Nina. A sign of a step up and away, into a now mythic past of lace tablecloths and turbaned servants in their grandparents' spacious homes in Bangalore. Long before they knew the ache of waking into mornings in which each moment could be counted like a heartbeat or on fingers without end, without relief of cessation. Together they sit, waiting, around the table. The clock is moving backwards toward a frozen moment. If they could, they would reach out all at once and still the clock.

The child is still asleep, the chandeliers brightly lit to vaporize the darkness, when Siddharth finally says what Nina has been dreading.

"There is no one there."

He reaches out to hold her hand, trying to find a way into this conversation, attempting an apology perhaps. Nina pulls away, a gesture unrehearsed and awkward, and he looks askance and drums his fingers lightly. This man has neither the means nor the capacity to speak, or any right to reconvene the unforgiven world. He has a wife called Laurie and a house with a swimming pool. He has watched Nina direct and caution the afternoon air; he has exchanged knowing glances with his wife. He has never conjured up a German weatherman. He has never traced the landscape of a crumpled pillow. He has borne and lost the sense of falling black debris. And here they are so many years later around a kitchen table in the shadow of a child now dispersed in the wind, light as ash, lost, floating free.

"Maya," says Nina sharply, and it is the only time she will speak their daughter's name. Siddharth is quiet in his chair, Laurie stricken.

Seven years now, a breath in time. A child, ten-almost-eleven, rushing downstairs in the morning, waving goodbye from the driveway in her color-sprinkled coat. "Watch me go! Count to ten, Mom! Ready, set. . . . Wait, count to hundred!" In moments she'd turn the corner, run up the road, step onto a yellow school bus, "See you later, Mom!" and the day picks up its daily drumming, beats out its implacable routines. Three o'clock, a school bus turns the bend, but it doesn't stop, not this time. She wasn't at my place this afternoon, says Jenny. She missed her lesson, says the clarinet instructor. Not to worry, soothe the neighbors, these things rarely happen. Perhaps she's at another friend's house. Perhaps at the library. The flurry then, of police and urgent Amber Alerts, of social workers and news reporters. The day freezes, becomes its own mausoleum. And the months, the years, founder in this silent purity of an absence vast and virginal as newly fallen snow.

At this moment, unmoored to any other, Nina sees that Siddharth's will to speak now is a step toward reprieve. An attempt to recover and let go, as if they were not creatures caught in amber, stilled in their entrancements. To venture every movement as if wagering answers, to let one cross the other out, to nullify and walk away. They will stay in touch—though in truth they were never very far apart. In the days after their daughter's disappearance, they were almost lovers once again, until the waiting dried out, fell into a drought redeemed only by despair. But if the earth is forever riven, the years ahead are now turned and ready, damp for planting—if only she will offer benediction and wise counsel, give the word.

Nina gets up from the table and says that she is tired, it's been a long journey.

She walks into the third square bedroom where once a child might lie, her hair a pillow of brown bunting, not a shroud. Nina sees and does not see the sleeping child. There is no one there.

On the night plane back to South Bend, Nina is comforted by her indiscretion: she has stolen the pillow, tucked it in between her shoes and folded underthings. So soft and mushed, it could be a child burrowed in a suitcase.

Black ash is night or could be rain from blighted planes.

"Overhead bin, ma'am?" says the brightly smiling flight attendant. And up it goes.

The Texan in the seat next to her is benign, balding, lush with conversation.

"Trav'lin' alone?" he inquires, fussing with the arm rest.

It's not quite a pickup line.

The plane steadies for takeoff, the engines build into a rumble. For a moment she's suspended like a feather between earth and sky, like a cry without provenance or reception. Something rises in her, either grief or laughter. If she holds her breath she can begin counting, to ten or a hundred or forever. Nina looks through the aisle window but sees nothing but a square of black. The cabin lights are dimming, and in the darkness she's grateful not to see herself reflected.

Acknowledgments

My gratitude and thanks to:

Lisa Williams, editor of the New Poetry and Prose series, for her wise counsel and for giving these stories a place in the world.

Patrick O'Dowd, David Cobb, Jewell Boyd, and everyone at the University Press of Kentucky for their guidance in bringing the collection together. Ann Marlowe, for her close and insightful reading of the manuscript.

Ronald Spatz, Beth Staples, Alfredo De Palchi, Jodi Daynard, Lauralee Leonard, and Danielle Ofri, editors who published previous versions of these stories in their literary periodicals.

Alan Ross, who championed the work of writers, both established and unknown, in the canonical pages of *London Magazine.* In memoriam.

The Vermont Studio Center, for a space to write and build fellowship.

Vimala Arjun, Nayantara Krishanaa, Sudha Krishna Kumar, Preetpal Dahele, Elizabeth "Laji" Joseph, Geraldine Cooke, Michael Yetman, Margaret Moan Rowe, Padmini Balachandran, Savita Chandiramani, Veena Halady, Estelle Frankl, Pat Clark, Linnea Vacca, K. Prabhavathi,

Acknowledgments

Joanna Sizmur, Suchitra Sadanandan, Rajni Badlani, V. Saraswathi, Max Westler, Gita and Nandita Divakaran, Mary Burget, and Juana Celia Djelal, for lighting up moments along the way.

Silwat Khan Pedersen, in remembrance of her laughter and fearless irreverence.

K. Kuttikrishna Menon, Madhavi Menon, and Kalyani Nayar, for the stability of a provenance that reaches across migrations and time.

Krishna Kumar, *mon frère bien-aimé, mon ami,* for charting the road so selflessly.

Achan, who conjured up magic from fairy tales and Shakespeare; Amma, in whose gentle spirit my whole world rested. All that I write is in your honor.

Nitin, and our children, Avi, Ro, and Taran, without whose love and joyful presence in my life there would be no book. Every journey begins with you.

* * *

These stories first appeared in the following publications, some as shorter versions and under different titles:

Alaska Quarterly Review, "Simulacra"
Bellevue Literary Review, "Almost Theides"
Boston Review, "Home Fires"
Chelsea, "The Secret Women of Vietnam"
London Magazine, "Temporary Shelters" (as "Summer Crossing"), "Chiaroscuro" (as "Optics")
Malahat Review, "The Bonny Hills of Scotland" (as "Speaking of Bunty")
O. Henry Festival Stories, reprint of "Home Fires"
Shenandoah, "Triptych, with Interruptions"
Words and Images (University of Southern Maine), "The Gentle Cycle"

THE UNIVERSITY PRESS OF KENTUCKY
NEW POETRY AND PROSE SERIES

This series features books of contemporary poetry and fiction that exhibit a profound attention to language, strong imagination, formal inventiveness, and awareness of one's literary roots.

SERIES EDITOR: Lisa Williams

ADVISORY BOARD: Camille Dungy, Rebecca Morgan Frank, Silas House, Davis McCombs, and Roger Reeves

Sponsored by Centre College

 CENTRE
COLLEGE